WHAT ARE YA?

WHAT ARE YA?

JENNY PAUSACKER

ANGUS
& ROBERTSON
PUBLISHERS

The author wishes to acknowledge the assistance
of the Literature Board of the Australia Council.

Creative writing programme
assisted by the Literature
Board of the Australia Council,
the Federal Government's arts
funding and advisory body.

ANGUS & ROBERTSON PUBLISHERS

Unit 4, Eden Park, 31 Waterloo Road,
North Ryde, NSW, Australia 2113, and
16 Golden Square, London W1R 4BN,
United Kingdom

First published in Australia
by Angus & Robertson Publishers in 1987
First published in the United Kingdom
by Angus & Robertson (UK) in 1987

© Copyright Jenny Pausacker 1987

National Library of Australia
Cataloguing-in-publication data.

Pausacker, Jenny.
  What are ya?

  ISBN 0 207 15366 3.

  I. Title.

A823'.3

Printed in China

To Andy and Diana for friendship and stories; to Beryl for getting me thinking; to the young women's group "What Are Ya?" for letting me share the name; and thanks to everyone who gave comments along the way.

CONTENTS

CAST OF CHARACTERS

Barb's group
Barb O'Connell
Silvana Angostello
Debbie Ralton

Barb's family
Sandra O'Connell, Barb's mother
Sue O'Connell, Barb's sister
Mr and Mrs Hartwell, Barb's grandparents
Barry, Mrs O'Connell's boyfriend

Leith's group
Leith Dunbar
Trina Dunbar, Leith's cousin
Pam Wagner
Karen Swallow

Leith's family
Neil Dunbar, Leith's father

Xenia's group
Xenia Anastasiou
Paul Anastasiou, Xenia's twin
Mark Douglas
Cass Rosenbloom

Also at Central High School
Gavin Petty
Con Theostratis
Mr Hansen
Miss Vincini
Mrs Simons   } teachers
Ms Lee

1
BARB AND LEITH

Central High School is the way it sounds — inner city. Tall grey concrete slabs arm-wrestle for space on a tiny block of land, with a mural, a few dying trees and some graffiti about the under-eighteen dole round the edges.

It was one of the few warm winter days, and the kids were desperate to get out into the sunshine. As soon as the siren went, they mobbed the corridors, yelling to each other.

"Dunno if I can last a whole year of it."

"You're not wrong."

Barb O'Connell was pushing her way through the mob to find Leith Dunbar when she ran into a pile-up. Gavin Petty and Con Theostratis were blocking the doorway with their bags and bodies.

"If you don't mind," Barb said to the back of Gavin's neck. He jumped, and Con caught him off guard and sent him sprawling. Barb slid neatly between them.

"Watch y'manners in front of ladies, Gav," jeered Con. Gavin swung a punch at his upper arm, and Barb turned and gave a quick two-finger salute before she went on, straight-backed, down the crowded ramp.

"That chick is up herself," complained Con.

"Ah, she's all right."

"Fancy her, do you?"

"Not half as much as you fancy yourself," said Gavin smartly.

Barb stopped to make sure Silvana Angostello was going to the pub that night, and Con and Gavin fought their way out into the street. Gavin paused to pull his foot out of someone's school bag, and looked up into a silent stare from Leith Dunbar.

"Pardon me for living," he muttered, unnerved for a moment. Con moved in, hitching at his jeans.

"What you reading?"

Leith's broad shoulders hunched in on themselves. She held up the book, still silent.

"*Bleak House*. No wonder you're so bloody happy," grinned Con, looking her up and down. "Any sexy bits? You can read them out to me, hey?"

"You wouldn't like it." Leith's voice started out low, then jumped to a light tenor.

"Give us a go. I'm very sensitive, y'know, when I'm not mucking around with this moron here." Gavin shoved Con, and he leaned in at Leith. "Come on, try me."

Leith's face tightened, and she stared silently on.

"Oh, Jesus, not you two again," said Barb over her shoulder.

Con smoothed back his thick springy hair. "Sorry to disappoint you, we were just going."

"I'll live."

They swaggered away, posing like heroes for the year nine girls, then breaking off to scuffle with each other. Barb laughed: Leith tucked her book away tidily, her face still tight.

"Hey," said Barb, noticing, "don't let them get to you. Just look them in the eye and go, 'What are ya?' or something. It only encourages them if you go all quiet."

"Yeah."

"Con's all right. For a maniac."

"Yeah."

Halfway down the street Leith realised with horror that the tidy cottages, their brass numbers and their clumps of bamboo, had all blurred. She blinked hard at the giveaway tears, but she kept on remembering what they had told her about big roaming dogs — "Don't let on you're scared." She was still scared, just the same.

"You take things too seriously," Barb warned her.

"You reckon?" asked Leith hopefully. "So how do I stop?"

"You don't start."

Barb leaned back and enjoyed the big room — the ceiling rose with its plaster flowers and fruit, the curtains patterned with birds and strawberries, the little courtyard outside the long window, the tall bookcases, the brown corduroy armchairs. She wanted all of it, but she knew how much all of it cost.

Mr Dunbar carried in a wooden tray crowded with coffee percolator, brown cups and cake plate. He was a small man, just under Leith's height, but bony where she was solid, with restless big-knuckled hands and watchful eyes under a fringe of sandy-grey hair.

"Help yourself," he said. "Go on, have both," as Barb's hand hovered between a macaroon and an almond biscuit. "You girls are all too thin. I like a woman to have a bit of flesh on her bones."

"Like me," said Leith, pulling her windcheater away from where it outlined her breasts and midriff. "I should go on a diet."

"There's something very suspicious about diets," began Mr Dunbar, settling into an armchair; and he was away on one of his theories. Leith interrupted with theories of her own, but Barb just sat back, sipping real coffee and smoothing the brown corduroy. She liked listening to Mr Dunbar—he was even better than suave Mr Hansen at Central. If she lived here, maybe she would have views about everything too.

"We've got to get those books."

Leith stood up suddenly, and her father looked up at her, the light picking out the hollows under his eyes and cheekbones. Leith felt mean about leaving him, but then he said, "Yes, I've got some work to do before tea," and she decided she must have imagined the sad look.

As she clattered up the stairs, she called back to Barb, "So how d'you stop yourself brooding about things?"

"I brood sometimes."

"Not as much as me, you don't."

"No-one broods as much as you, Leith Dunbar." Barb plumped down on Leith's bed. "You think about every little thing that happens to you—what the teachers say, what I say, what Con Theostratis says. If I thought that much, I'd never do anything."

"I'd rather think," Leith defended herself.

"You could do both, y'know."

Leith felt jumpy and shot off to find the books she had

promised. Barb studied her—tall, blonde, solid legs, solid body, unexpectedly long fragile neck stooped to hide her height, unexpectedly expressive face once you got past the heavy eyebrows and the definite nose.

"I wish you'd let me pick some clothes for you, just for once."

"You might as well give up on that," said Leith with a grin. "I don't have your kind of style."

Barb sighed for her own pale skin, pale freckles, pale brown hair, medium height—but style, yes, she did have style.

"It's such a waste. I could do heaps with your natural advantages. I wish I was tall."

Leith's grin got wider. "And I'd give you eight centimetres with pleasure. Maybe that's the secret of our success as friends—we both admire what each other's got."

Barb sighed. "Maybe."

As he drove Barb home, Mr Dunbar explained the philosophy lecture he was writing. She concentrated hard as a way of avoiding his driving, which swung between reckless and ultra-cautious. Outside the car window rows of renovated terrace houses gave way to renovated workers' cottages, and then rows of unrenovated workers' cottages, including the one where she lived.

Barb let herself in at the front door and was instantly hit with TV sounds and dinner smells. In the lounge her grandma, little and round as a mouse in a picture book, was explaining a quiz show to her grandad, who nodded quietly. Sue sprawled across a shabby armchair, kicking her feet irritably.

"Some guy rang for you, but I forgot his name," she told the air.

"Thanks. I'll do the same for you one day."

Barb dodged into the kitchen before her sister could work that one out. Her mum was cooking tea, leaning against the stove as if she might have fallen without it. When she turned round, her bright hair and careful make-up kept her face looking young, but the droop of tiredness was getting to her mouth.

"Let me do that. You go and watch TV."

"Don't you have homework, Barb?"

"Yeah, but I got all weekend . . ."

"Go on. You'll fit in half an hour at least, before you go out on the town."

Barb kissed her mum extra hard on the cheek as a compromise, and got a friendly push out the back door. As she scrunched down the path to the grey fibro bungalow that filled half the back yard, she found herself redesigning her grandparents' house for the hundredth time. Skylights everywhere, a glass wall at the back, you could do wonders with the kitchen and bathroom: but there still wouldn't be enough bedrooms to go round. And it still wouldn't look like Leith's house.

She switched on the light and the bungalow crowded in on her. It was her bedroom by night and her grandad's workroom by day, so there was an old double bed in the corner next to a heavy cupboard, then her grandad's massive desk under the window and benches everywhere, stacked with the silver cups, trophies and shields that her grandad engraved by hand. Barb made her regular check of the piece he was working on. She had slept with the Melbourne Cup for a week last year, but today there was only a fairly ordinary shield with kangaroos and emus peering out from a coating of green wax.

Barb settled down at the desk and a great first paragraph for her maths assignment came whole into her mind. She scribbled it down, then read out the last sentence to admire it.

"Talking to yourself. You've gone mental," said Sue through the window.

"Some people wouldn't recognise homework if they were trapped in a lift with it."

Sue pulled a face. "It's not fair, goody-goody, you out here in the bungalow where you could do whatever you like, and me stuck in the same room as mum, with her watching every single thing I do."

"Be a slackarse then. You'll end up with no job and be stuck here forever."

"Won't," said Sue in a baby voice. "I'll go and live in Mum and Barry's house near the hills and have a big room all to myself."

"That's what you think."

"What d'you mean?" Sue scowled.

"They have to get married first, don't they?"

"They're gonna, fishface, any minute. Barry's just sorting things out."

"With his wife."

"He's sorting things out," yelled Sue, her spiky hair bristling. "Anyway, I'm still not speaking to you," she remembered, and slouched off down the path to the loo.

Barb slammed the window shut and re-read her paragraph. It looked pretty stupid this time. She had used a word she had found in the dictionary, and Mr Hansen would realise she was putting it on — not like Leith, who used long words because she thought that way. She would fail. She would never get into year 12, let alone teacher training after that. She would end up on the dole, or in some dead-end job, bored every day and tired every night.

Barb started to count her grandad's engraving tools, hanging in a row before her like rubber stamps, but with differently shaped blades below the round handles. She was on her fifth time through and the panic was starting to die down, when Mrs O'Connell called, "Phone!"

"Not Danny again?" Hasn't he got the message yet? thought Barb automatically.

"No, he says his name's Claudio."

Claudio, she wondered, then remembered last Friday at the pub. Claudio! She must have made an impression after all.

Barb pushed her homework aside and raced to the phone.

2
FRIDAY NIGHT

"Now we've just got time to go to Myers before the film starts," said Trina.

Trina Dunbar, Leith's cousin, had bullied them all into going to the city with her for late night shopping, because her boyfriend Jeff was working. Leith felt tired out already. Trina kept wanting her to try on clothes; Pam Wagner kept wanting to get her aside and ask if she thought Mark Douglas was somewhere in the city; Karen Swallow, who hated shops, kept wanting to spar with her.

"Well, come on," said Trina impatiently.

Swallow stopped in her tracks. "No, thanks. I've seen enough bloody shirts to last me ten years." She planted her small stocky body as firmly as a boxer and glared at Trina, her green-brown eyes glittering against pale skin and dusky close-cropped hair.

Trina puffed out a sigh from round rosy cheeks. "Don't be difficult, Swallow. I just have to pick up this dress I've got on lay-by—it's for Jeff's sister's twenty-first."

"So pick it up," shrugged Swallow. "Me and Leith'll meet you back here."

Pam's round eyes looked from Trina to Leith, undecided, till Trina whisked her away.

"Good," said Swallow with satisfaction. "I hate all that female stuff."

"Female yourself."

"Not like *that*, anyway. Come on, I want to see the buskers."

The main difference between being hauled around by Trina and being hauled around by Swallow was that they hauled her in different directions. One or other of them had been telling her what to do ever since she had arrived at Central.

Leith sighed emptily. At least when Janelle had been around, they could catch each other's eye and grin whenever Trina or

Swallow got particularly bossy. But Janelle had left last year to work in her uncle's shop, and Pam Wagner was useless; all she wanted to do was talk about Mark Douglas as much as possible. Altogether, year 11 was an ace number one drag.

Swallow grabbed at her sleeve. "Get that lot — a whole bunch of women wearing jeans and singing madrigals! Let's have a listen."

Leith, who was tone-deaf, watched Swallow's face instead. As she listened to the music, her eyes went serious, her mouth softened. Leith was wishing she could introduce herself to this serious Swallow, when she was distracted by Silvana Angostello, who waved her over to the side of the mall.

"Guess what? My sister Maria just had her baby," she announced proudly.

Leith wondered what she was supposed to say. "Is she pleased?"

"Of course she is." Silvana widened her glossy brown eyes. "Don't you like babies?"

"Dunno. Not much. Why should I?"

Silvana shook her head. "Oh, Leith." She paused to give Leith a chance to understand everything she couldn't put into words, and Leith frowned doggedly back. "Trust you to have a different opinion from everyone else," laughed Silvana, and away she went.

Stranded at the edge of the mall, Leith kept on arguing to herself. So why did everyone have to like the same things anyway? Babies, summer, sport, clothes, guys. All as boring as hell. Leith was feeling larger and more awkward every second, so she went and hid in the crowd round the nearest buskers.

Four kids dressed as punk-style tramps were belting out a song about unemployment. The second in the line was Xenia Anastasiou from Central. She's brave, thought Leith, as Xenia strutted up and down, all dash and angles, her dark eyes flicking across the crowd and forcing them to see the point of the song. In the break she tugged her black curls with a long bony hand while she argued furiously with the others. She's really alive, sighed Leith, and wondered if Xenia had noticed her.

Then a hand slid into her pocket, and she spun round to find Swallow gleefully waving her paperback. Leith made an angry grab, Swallow darted away and they wrestled in the middle of the mall. Leith wanted to swat Swallow like a mosquito and go back to Xenia, but instead she found herself blurting out, "What d'you think about babies, Swallow?"

Swallow straightened her windcheater and raised her wispy eyebrows. "I've got a niece," she said in the deep growl that could make simple remarks sound funny. "Every time I pick her up, she pisses herself, or worse. The feeling's mutual."

Leith grinned, feeling better. Trina and Pam came up, so she asked them too. Trina creased her shiny forehead.

"Well, they're so small and helpless, I s'pose we've got an instinct to take care of them. Haven't you ever felt moved, looking at those tiny hands and feet?"

Leith was interested in spite of herself, but Swallow clutched at her stomach. "Moved to spew," she agreed. "All right, Pammy, it's your turn." Pam stared back like a rabbit caught in headlights. "Come on, it's simple, d'you like little babies? Yes or no? What would you say if Marvellous Mark offered you one?"

Pam turned on her heel and walked away.

"You don't have to be unpleasant, Swallow," said Trina severely, "just because you and Pam have different views."

We didn't get as far as talking about views, Trina. We never do. Leith went straight into a dream of friends who liked to talk and share ideas and find out more about each other. Maybe at uni, she told herself hopefully, but that's a year and a half away, how can I wait till then?

Meanwhile she had caught up with Pam by mistake. She tried to think of something to say.

"Xenia Anastasiou was busking in the mall."

Pam looked up with quick interest. "Xenia? She's a friend of Mark's. Was he there too?"

Barb sipped her drink and watched Claudio over the shining edge of the glass. You had to say he was good-looking; plus he dressed smartly; plus he always had something to say. Right now he was joking with Silvana and her boyfriend Craig as if he had known them all his life, instead of for the last few hours. Maybe he's the one, thought Barb as he held out his arm and she slid into its smooth leather curve. But a part of her stayed out there, watching.

Debbie Ralton bounced through a gap in the crowd, orange hair standing on end, cheeks pink from dancing, wide mouth still wider round a grin, and Barb yelled, "What's the joke?"

"Just danced with a nerd, and saw a real spunk in the distance. Story of my life."

"Short story."

"Not if you repeat it a hundred times. Hey, there he goes."

Barb could only see a streak of darkness against a spotlight, but she whistled encouragingly.

"I saw him first," yelled Debbie.

"It's all right, I brought my own."

"Your own what?" Claudio's breath brushed her ear.

"My own spunk," Barb called back, tightening her arm round his waist as he kissed her ear lobe.

"Ah, save it till later, you two!" shouted Debbie, and dived back into the crowd.

Barb turned slowly till her eyes were level with Claudio's, and they searched each other's faces. She liked this stage, showing you were keen enough to make it worth their while, but not so keen that they were going to have it all their own way. As Claudio's mouth closed down on hers, she kissed back lightly and swiftly curled round to snuggle against his shoulder.

"What's Deb up to?" called Silvana.

"She's seen a spunk."

"Another one." Silvana rolled her eyes.

"Maybe this'll be different."

"Come off it. Debbie's not planning to settle for any one guy. It'd spoil her fun."

"Do I spoil your fun, Silv?" Craig yelled down the table.

"Sure do. I really miss hanging round with stupid little boys. Look, there's Con and Gavin, pissed out of their brains. They're animals."

Barb looked. She knew half the people in the room, but the flashing lights and shadows, the shiver of the music sent them spinning past as fast as a video clip. That guy's body, that girl's crazy gear: maybe not so special if you got a long hard look at them, but all part of the scene. There wasn't much you could do about the way you were at school: but at least there was Friday night.

Then Con and Gavin swayed into view, knocking glasses off three tables at once. Barb curled her lip. They might have muscles like men under the tight T-shirts, but they carried on like kids. It was true what people said, girls matured faster than boys.

She turned thankfully back to Claudio, but he was busy slinging off at the band with his younger brother Vince, who was in year 12 at Central. Then, when Silvana came out of a long clinch with Craig, Claudio called to her, "Bet your folks'd love a snapshot of that."

Silvana looked back through a fringe of dark eyelashes. "If my dad comes in with a shotgun, I'm with you, okay?"

"Sure thing, us Italians stick together."

Barb felt a warning stab. Then Craig called to her, "And if *my* dad comes in with a shotgun, I'm with you, not this wog here, okay?" and it turned into a four-way flirt.

But I must be pretty interested in Claudio if I can get jealous over Silvana, Barb noted. After all, she and Craig were really in love. Even when they talked to other people, their hands still reached out and touched and wound together. It could be all right, thought Barb; feeling like that. As long as you were sure.

Debbie elbowed her way back to the table. "Barb, I got to get onto that dance floor. Be a sport — he'd have to feel sorry for two chicks dancing together."

"Probably think you were lesos," Claudio warned. "Take Vince—anyone would feel sorry for a girl who was dancing with him."

Debbie dragged Vince away while his brother laughed. "That chick is crazy."

"She's a real goer."

"Yeah, yeah, I like her all right. Like you better, though."

"Well, that's lucky, 'cause you're out with me."

"I reckon I am lucky at that," said Claudio. "I'm with a girl who's pretty and clever and good fun. What more could a man want?"

Barb's smile said, "Nothing," but not in words, so it wasn't boasting. Claudio put his arm round her proudly and started to talk cars with Craig.

On the dance floor Debbie clicked and swayed round a hardly-moving Vince, making the most of the space before the main band came on. Bands of blue light gleamed down her solid lycra thighs; light touched her outstretched arms and round breasts and ruffled her hennaed hair as she nodded energetically. For a moment she almost convinced Barb that the support band was playing well.

And for a moment she almost envied Debbie for being so up-front, going for what she wanted and not tying herself down. But I couldn't joke about the knockbacks like Deb does, Barb reminded herself. I can't stand failure.

The music stopped, leaving an echo of decibels in her ears that was almost like silence, though everyone was still shouting their heads off. Cool Fools' roadies started to shift mikes and amps, and Barb's feet started to tap. This was what she had come for. Good music and good dancing.

"Enjoying yourself?"

"Tell them to start playing," Barb demanded.

"Tell them yourself. I've got something else I've been wanting to do for a while," said Claudio.

Barb came out of the long dark kiss into whirling lights, green, red, purple, yellow. Cool Fools in their big ragged diamond-patterned shirts struck guitars and drums right on cue as she opened her eyes, then launched into their hit song, a punk version of "Why do fools fall in love?"

So she went from kissing to dancing, very smooth, and on the way she noticed Silvana and Craig wrapped round each other, and Debbie parading before a definite spunk. Everyone was happy.

Leith closed her book and turned off her bedside light, and the memories of the day came and pressed down on her chest, one after the other. Trina and Barb wanting to change the way she dressed, and Silvana saying she was different from everyone else. Con leaning at her and Swallow punching her in the ribs, and her twisting away from being touched. Her father's hollow face and Pam walking away: sadness, all the sadness.

Just as she got one thought steady, another came and jostled it away. Now Barb was saying, "You can think *and* act, y'know." I can't, Leith insisted, I can't even keep track of everything, as it is. Like Trina and Pam and Swallow: if she really admitted she didn't like hanging round with them, she'd have to do something about it. But what?

Back came the picture of the friends who talked and shared ideas and found out more about each other; and this time one of the faces was Barb's, and one was Xenia's.

But Barb and I do talk after school, Leith told herself. There was no point wanting more. She might feel reallest when she was with Barb, but Barb had dozens of people — Debbie, Silvana, the guys she went out with — so that was that, okay? She had to get away from that thought, so she went to Xenia.

What if Xenia wanted to be her friend, and they went places together, and talked about everything? For a moment Xenia was there and clear beside her — tall and spindly, melting eyes, inquiring nose. Then, with an effort, Leith sent her away. She's brave and alive, and I'm — I'm — what are ya? she jeered in the darkness as she started to cry again, smothering her sobs in the pillow.

I'm nothing. I don't know what to say, or I say too much. I don't know what to feel, I can't even remember Mum. I'm different, just like Silvana said.

3
GETTING THE ENGAGED SIGNAL

Pam was telling Leith how her friend Heather had let her down — going out with a guy from work, instead of doing the pinball parlours with her to see if Mark Douglas was there. Leith had said the wrong thing three times, so now she was just nodding.

Then Trina sailed down the corridor, Swallow bobbing along behind her. "Mind yourself with that bag," Trina called severely to Gavin Petty. "You could put a little kid's eye out, y'know."

"Yes, miss," jeered Gavin, but he swung the bag off his shoulder as he raced on.

Trina came to a triumphant halt in front of Leith and Pam, her freckles gleaming, her copper hair shivering with pleasure. "I've got some news for you two."

"You'll never guess," added Swallow at her elbow.

"Jeff and I've decided. We're getting engaged on my birthday, three weeks after the exams."

"See? Aren't you surprised?" Swallow asked Leith.

"I just can't take it in."

They stood and giggled while Pam sighed, "You lucky thing," and Trina started to describe her plans for the engagement party.

"But you won't be invited, Swallow, unless you behave yourself," she said, half joking.

"No probs," said Swallow, still grinning. "I won't be coming anyway."

Trina stared, open-mouthed, and Swallow dug her hands deeper into her pockets. "Wouldn't be fair," she explained. "I'll never get married m'self, so you'd never get a return invite."

Oh wow! thought Leith. Her eyes ranged secretly round the group. Swallow staring coolly at Trina, her face a deliberate blank. Pam looking from Trina to Swallow as if she was at a tennis match. And Trina laughing gently at Swallow's little joke.

"You'll feel differently one day, Swallow," she said, shaking her head.

Leith's excitement drained away. That's it, she mourned. Don't ever again think these people will discuss anything. She took a last hopeful look at Swallow, who swung a playful punch.

"Coming to English or not, kid?"

"Nothing better to do."

Morning recess was nearly over, but the Dungeons and Dragons players were still hard at it, dice rolling, voices rising, words like "sword of power", "goblin attack" and "dark waters of the underground river" echoing off the grey bricks. A few kids hung around watching them.

"What d'you get out of it?" asked Con Theostratis curiously.

"It stimulates the imagination, if you know what that means," snapped Xenia Anastasiou. "Now piss off."

"Bloody leso," Con grumbled to Debbie. "They're weirdos, that lot."

"Yeah. I played D&D once. Too much like homework."

"Better stick to Space Invaders. Pow, pow!" Con snapped her bra strap twice, and Debbie pulled away, swearing.

Leith tapped her watch, and Pam mouthed back, "Just a minute," and went on gazing at Mark Douglas. He crouched over the game like a football player, muscled arms, loose powerful hands, guarded eyes. Typical jock, thought Leith—except when you knew he put out a small poetry magazine in his spare time.

"Jesus, Paul, we've found half a dozen gold cups in the last few months. Can't you think of something more original?"

Xenia's powerful voice rode over everyone, but then Paul, her twin, made everyone stop and listen to his soft mutterings. Tall and lanky like Xenia, he was somehow more blurry, slouched in the big derro overcoat that was his trademark, his olive skin pitted, his long-lashed eyes always directed at his feet. A dag, but all the same even his school jumper, too tight and unravelling at the edges, made him look more like a crim than a kid.

"That's it for the moment anyway," he mumbled. Xenia grabbed at his sleeve as he swept up the dice.

"Hang about. You can't leave us there."

"I'm the Dungeon Master."

"Dungeon Hitler, more like." Xenia's eyes flashed to the others for support. Mark Douglas just started to pack up his books, but Cass Rosenbloom smiled back.

"Yeah, I know, Xenia, but Vincini will kill you if you're late again."

"Bugger Vincini."

Cass stood up and held out her hand. Next to angular Xenia she was drawn from circles—round cheeks, round breasts, round hips, round waves in her yellow hair, round blue eyes. Imagine a thirties movie star, thought Leith. Then add an orange shirt and a black tie, spiky eyelashes, black nail polish and blue stripes in the hair, and that's Cass.

Xenia let herself be hauled up, grumbling all the way. As they started down the corridor Pam put on a burst of speed and tugged at Paul's elbow.

"About that gold cup, Leith could help. She knows about legends and that stuff."

Paul bent his head towards Leith. "Yeah?"

She gritted her teeth and gave Pam a filthy look. "Oh well, there's the Tarnhelm, a sort of Viking helmet with wings, made you invisible. That's out of Norse myth."

"Tarnhelm," repeated Paul. "Good-o. Thanks," and he took off again.

"You could've said a bit more," whispered Pam reproachfully. "They might have asked us to join, or something."

"You could have said a bit less," snapped Leith. "Do your own dirty work next time," and she turned sharply into the classroom ahead of Pam.

Miss Vincini, frostily elegant as usual in her charcoal trousers, pale grey jumper, iron grey hair, was giving the class a pep talk. Leith wasn't worried about the exams, a whole term away, so she sat and wondered why she wasn't sorry for snapping at Pam, when normally she would be. Maybe she was getting tough.

Miss Vincini moved on to the reading for the term project, which Leith had almost finished. She thought about Dungeons and Dragons instead. It looked like a great game, but Paul and Mark and Cass were even scarier than Xenia; she couldn't imagine joining anything they were in. Then her heart was beating faster, and she *was* imagining it—telling Paul about myths, watched admiringly by Xenia and the others. "Wow, Leith, how d'you know all that?" Blushing, she tuned back in to the lesson.

Miss Vincini's light eyes, magnified behind gold-rimmed glasses, were fixing the class like specimens as she reminded them about deadlines and no extensions. Xenia's hand rocketed up, and someone hissed, "There goes bigmouth."

"Miss Vincini," declaimed Xenia, "I won't be able to do any work that weekend. The youth theatre group I'm in, we've got dress rehearsals."

"In that case, your project had better be finished before the weekend, hadn't it?"

Xenia sprawled back at her desk. "Let's face it, we've got wall-to-wall homework these days. I'll need an extension."

The teacher looked politely surprised. "When I give three weeks' notice, I don't give extensions. I thought I'd made that clear."

"But I have to have one," Xenia explained. "You don't understand, this play's more important than *homework*."

"That's quite enough, Xenia. You'll submit the project on the due date, or you'll fail."

"It's not fair! You can't fail me, my dad will be livid, he—"

"Xenia!" Miss Vincini adjusted her narrow shoulders and long hands a fraction, to make it clear that she might explode any second. She watched Xenia into silence, then swept her eye across the rest of the class, who had mostly drifted off into their own thoughts or conversations.

"Now, if we can get back to the parliamentary system . . ."

As Miss Vincini went on with the lesson, Leith heard a loud sniff. She looked round. Xenia was slumped heavily on her desk. Tears fell unashamedly from her red-rimmed eyes as she sniffed again.

Leith's head swung back as if she were riding a punch. Her hands twitched, she wanted to block her ears. Instead she fixed her eyes on the teacher, but though she could take in her words one by one, she couldn't get them to make sentences. She was waiting the whole time for the next sniff to echo through the classroom, half believing she could hear the soft plop of the falling tears. Time slowed to a crawl. There was nothing in the world except the roaring in Leith's ears and the small clear sounds of Xenia crying.

As Miss Vincini finally started to pack up her books, Cass leapt forward. "Look, I just wanted to explain how Xenia's theatre group isn't just some kids' thing, they get really good reviews, so—"

Leith missed the rest, charging down the corridor red-faced, bumping into shoulders and locker doors, getting out.

"Days like this, I'd just like to get up and walk out of class in to the sunshine and never come back." Debbie stretched out her arms to the blue sky, and Silvana giggled.

"Where would you go—over to a certain garage not far away, to talk a certain spunky mechanic into wagging it too?"

"Nah, I'd pinch my brother's motorbike and set off round Australia. Don't you ever get sick of school?"

"Once a day, at least. Only reason I'm here is, my folks think if I spend half my life at school, then I'll get these big deal chances they never got. Crazy," sighed Silvana. "I just want the chance to be happy with Craig, like Mum is with Dad."

"Tell 'em how even kids with HSC are sitting home on their bums, watching midday movies and waiting for their dole cheques."

"Shut up, Deb, or I'll go walking out into the sunshine looking for a motorbike," groaned Barb.

"Ah, you'll be right, you're a brain, not like me and Silv here."

"No way. Brains are like Leith, or Paul Anastasiou's lot."

"They're superbrains," said Debbie smartly, flipping a sandwich crust at her. "You work, Barb O'Connell, don't deny it."

"Can't get out of it. Mum's on at me the whole time about, 'You need an education, so you can support yourself, you never know what will happen.' S'pose she's got a point."

"Ha. That Claudio could support me, any time. What's he like, then?"

"Okay." Barb drooped her eyelids, and Debbie laughed.

"You're so bloody sure of yourself. Wish I was like you."

Barb's jaw nearly dropped in surprise. Quickly, she said the first thing that came into her head.

"Heard about Trina Dunbar? Thinks she's the only person who ever got engaged."

"Soon will be," said Debbie idly. "*Girl* reckons in future everyone will live together first, then get married."

"Tell that to my dad," said Silvana. "Then run."

They laughed. "It makes sense, though," said Debbie. "My sister lived with this guy before Russell—said it was the only way she could have found out what an arsehole he was."

The siren went. As they crossed the road back to Central, Silvana asked, "Didn't Russell mind? I mean, *living* with someone . . ."

"It's okay, Silv, you can get engaged to Craig, whatever *Girl* says," Barb soothed.

"Oh, we're not getting engaged—but that's cause my folks will go off their faces. So we'll just tell them when we're getting married, and that way they'll only go off their faces once."

"Simple."

"Well, it is. Why are you laughing at me?"

Debbie shrugged her plump shoulders. "Probably cause we wish it was that simple for us, hey, Barb?"

"You're not wrong, Deb."

"I saw you today," Barb told Leith after school, "belting down the corridor like a bat out of hell. What happened?"

Leith drew in a deep breath and started to let out all her fury at Xenia. "I just don't understand how someone our age can sit there bawling like a kid in bubs' grade," she finished up. "Vincini should've sent her to Mr Michaels."

"And made a martyr of her?"

"Oh yeah." Leith slowed down. "That's probably why she didn't. You're good on people, Barb. So—why does Xenia carry on like that?"

"Because she's Xenia. Why get your knickers in a twist about it?"

"Oh, I dunno."

Leith went silent for a while, so Barb started to pump her about Trina's engagement plans. By the end she was hanging onto a fence, weak with laughter.

"Two years to go, and she knows what they'll eat at the wedding reception! Mad. Jesus, Leith, why do you hang round with them?"

Leith went silent again, but this time it was to think. "Trina's my cousin. And I quite like Swallow's sense of humour. It just sort of happened." She thought again. "At least they don't talk about boys all the time."

"Trina must."

"Nah, she talks about weddings and white goods and house payments."

"Real stimulating, not like talking about guys," said Barb sarcastically. "Honestly, you'd be better off with a loon like Xenia, even, than that lot."

"Have you done your history essay yet?" asked Leith. Barb took the hint, and they talked schoolwork till they parted at the corner.

Leith took a book out of her bag and read her way down the next block. She had perfected an inner radar that steered her away from passers-by and overhanging branches, and reading meant she couldn't think. But when she looked up to cross the road, Barb's voice chipped in again.

"Better off with Xenia."

Barb was usually right, but—. The anger ran through her again, except this time it carried with it a memory of Xenia's face, so vivid that Leith could have counted the tear-pointed eyelashes. Oh, damn her, thought Leith bitterly. I really admired her, and she's not like I imagined at all.

4
"IT'S UP TO YOU, BARB"

For a while Barb hoped Leith really would ditch Trina and the others—no way were they her sort. She even wondered if she should do something to steer Leith towards the Anastasiou crowd; they would be much better for her. But somehow she had never had much to do with Leith at school. Leith was far too innocent for her own good sometimes. Looking after her could turn into a full-time job.

Besides, she had other things to think about, like seeing a whole lot more of Claudio over the next few weeks. He was the best dancer she had ever come across, Barb decided, and Cool Fools was the best band. "Why do fools fall in love?" they sang out again, and Barb flicked towards Claudio as he balanced against her, then spun her into the next song. She felt like the fountain in the park, changing patterns without effort forever. Her hair was sticking to her forehead: she brushed it back and danced harder.

Walking out to the car, she still pulsed with music. The footpath felt as springy as a trampoline. She grabbed Claudio's arm to keep from falling, and he steadied her with a kiss.

In the neon-dappled darkness under the trees there were more kisses before they shifted into the back seat. Their bodies lazed easily together, soft and sleek from dancing. It's all smooth with Claudio, Barb approved. Not like these guys who go for a few target points and forget the rest.

She didn't stop his hand for a second as it travelled the length of her belly to play between her thighs. Barb rested against Claudio's shoulder. The neon glitter at the windows blurred and was swallowed up in darkness as she closed her eyes, and in the darkness she found the flashing lights of the dance floor, the electric taste of Claudio's mouth, the gentle shock of his fingers closing round her nipples. Barb shuddered at the memories, and as she did a dark and bright feeling ran a circle round her groin.

"Oh," she gasped in surprise, and hid her face in Claudio's jacket. She knew how to make herself feel that way, but somehow she'd never thought of it happening with a guy. Claudio held her for a while, lightly kissing her hair, then just as she was starting to relax, he said softly, "Want to?"

Barb had to think fast. Looking up with a drowsy smile, she murmured, "Wow, I couldn't, not after that. Do you mind?"

"That's fine," he said. "It's up to you, Barb."

A zipper buzzed, and he closed her hand round tight tender skin. It's only fair, Barb pointed out between strokes, he did the same to me. But another Barb, fully dressed, stayed on the far side of the seat and stuffed her fingers in her ears to drown out Claudio's deep private groans. I like him heaps better than Danny, she argued on. I really like him lots, but this part of things—I wish it was like dancing, where you don't have to think.

Her mum was asleep in front of the TV when she came in. Barb clattered saucepans in the kitchen for a few minutes and as she walked back into the lounge room Mrs O'Connell was rubbing her eyes dazedly.

"You got home early," said Barb.

"I didn't go out after all."

"Seeing Barry tomorrow then?"

"I'm not sure, he may come round in the evening. I feel like a bit of peace and quiet anyway. Work's been getting me down, and—"

Mrs O'Connell's sleepy face slackened; her eyes were damp. "The milk," said Barb quickly, and caught it halfway up the pan. Finding the Milo and stirring it in took a bit of time, and when she carried in the cups her mum was neat and composed as usual.

They cradled their drinks in silence for a while. Then Barb said, "What's the matter at work?" just as her mum said, "Did you have a nice night with Claudio?"

Barb wouldn't have minded talking about Claudio, but she waited, and finally Mrs O'Connell said, "Oh, nothing much, just the usual work problems, but I can't seem to get on top of them."

Barb could see it wouldn't be easy, getting used to an office again after fifteen years, but— "Is everything cool with you and Barry?" she asked.

Mrs O'Connell shifted the cup of Milo to a safer place on the chair arm. "Yes, of course, Barb. Barry has . . . has a few family commitments at the moment, but they'll soon be cleared up. Now, it must be late, we should both be in bed," she said in her most sensible voice.

All the way to the bungalow Barb counted the piles of books Barry had lent her over the last two years, the long discussions where he treated her as an adult. Without him she would never be slaving away to get into teachers college the year after next. But even when she had finished reminding herself how he was generous and encouraging and great to talk to, the fact remained: he still wasn't allowed to mess her mum around.

Barry didn't turn up on Saturday night either.

"A nice family evening," Mrs O'Connell said brightly, and got out the sewing machine. Against its steady zizz, clothes and sheets flew into piles all over the room, while Mrs O'Connell sat small and neat in the eye of the tornado.

Barb's grandparents took the portable TV into their bedroom, Mrs Hartwell clicking her tongue and shaking her head as she went. Sue disappeared to a friend's place, and Barb hung around to keep her mother company till Mrs O'Connell chased her off to finish her English assignment. She drew daisies down the margin for a while, thinking about Claudio at his family party thinking of her, then she tore up the page and started a new one.

Later, her brain full of sentences, Barb went back to the kitchen for a cup of coffee. The lounge was dark, but she looked in out of habit, and at the doorway stood a shadowy shape with a blind white face.

Barb's heart kicked abruptly against her chest. *Ghost, mummy, vampire.* Then Mrs O'Connell groped her way on down the passageway, and Barb blew out her fright, remembering the new oatmeal facepack. She giggled her way out into the blue night.

But all the time she worked, she kept seeing her mum, lying

flat on her back at the other end of the house, the oatmeal facepack hardening over the new tired lines on her face.

Barb helped her grandma wash up after lunch. It was Sue's turn, but she had walked out and gone to Maria's place.

"She's missing Barry," said Mrs Hartwell comfortably. "Thinks the sun shines out of him."

Barb glanced quickly to make sure the door was shut. "What d'you think of him, Nan?"

Her grandma tucked her mouth in. "Oh, he's charming enough when he wants to be, but he's still kept Sandra waiting nearly two years now."

"So is he trying to get out of it?" Barb asked directly.

"There's something going on. Barry hasn't missed Sunday lunch here for I don't know how long . . . Mind you, I'm sorry for his wife too, Barb. It isn't easy for a divorcee, even these days, and she's nearer Barry's age than your mother's."

Barb remembered her talk with Deb and Silv. "Maybe Mum and Barry should just live together."

Mrs Hartwell didn't answer, and Barb checked to see if she had shocked her, but her grandma was just staring thoughtfully at the lemon tree outside the window.

"What is it, Nan?"

"It's funny, I've never mentioned this to Sandra, but your grandfather and I — well, it was a while before we could get married, so we had a talk one day and decided there was no reason why we couldn't do some of the same things as if we were married."

"You —" Barb caught the next word in time, and went on goggling at her little round grandma, just as plump and proper in her navy dress as before she'd started talking about sex. "I didn't think you'd believe in that sort of thing."

"I don't approve of jumping into bed with every Tom, Dick and Harry, but that's because in my opinion it's the woman who pays. I knew Colin would stand by me if I got into trouble, and I suppose," Mrs Hartwell's small eyes opened wide and bright, "I suppose I thought, if I have to wait this long, I'd better make sure it's worth the wait." All her wrinkles danced like cat's whiskers round a smile. "Try before you buy," she said triumphantly.

"But what if you hadn't liked it?" Barb demanded.

"That wasn't a problem, as it turned out," said Mrs Hartwell happily. "But better to know, I'd say. Goodness me, I suppose I shouldn't be telling you all of this, but your mother's been on my mind lately. I'm glad you're a sensible girl who can take care of herself."

Sensible, sure of myself—boring, thought Barb, and shrugged. She was somewhere in between her mum, waiting years for Barry, and Debbie with a new guy each week. If that was sensible, she was stuck with it.

Mrs Hartwell had bustled off to put on the kettle, and Barb turned round with a dozen more questions about her mum, her dad, Barry, Claudio, herself. But her grandma was at the back door, calling her grandad in for a cup of tea, and the moment had gone.

Barb turned on her side to go to sleep, but ten minutes later she was lying on her back again, watching the shadows rippling across the ceiling. Nan and Grandad, it really worked for them, she marvelled. Her skin prickled, and Claudio's face floated towards her on the night, shining and handsome as a poster. Hold on, Barb warned, it mightn't work, you couldn't know in advance.

Pushing the sheet away, she wondered whether her mum and Barry were getting off. Maybe not. Maybe that's why they were having hassles.

So maybe she should get off with Claudio. Barb ran her hands up and down her front, noting flat stomach, neat waist, soft breasts. I could do it, she thought. I could have done it with Danny, only it's just never seemed worth it.

"It's the woman who pays," said Nan again, and Barb decided she was well on the way to brooding. She hitched up the blankets and rolled over again.

Anyway, I have to do it some time. Like Nan. Like Mum.

5
ANOTHER XENIA ANASTASIOU SHOW-OFF SCHEME

With classes and homework and dreams of Claudio, the week wheeled round to Friday again. Barb was planning what to wear when Leith nudged her.

"Got something to show you."

She looked really excited. Green hair colour, porno books, long earrings? No, none of that was really Leith's style, Barb decided.

"Where?" she hissed recklessly under Mrs Simons' nose.

Leith did an imitation of the perfect student till Mrs Simons went over to write on the board, when she hissed back, "Not here. The cemetery on the way home."

"The cemetery?" protested Barb.

"That's quite enough, Barb O'Connell," said Mrs Simons without turning round.

As she walked through the huge iron gates of the cemetery, Barb could see Claudio's dark opal eyes as he bent to kiss her; she tasted the sweet satin inside his lips. You're getting obsessed, she warned herself, and looked away at the rows of photos of Italian faces. They stared back across the banks of faded plastic flowers on the polished granite graves, and Barb blushed suddenly with relief. That's what got me thinking about Claudio Fantucci — talk about sick!

Leith hustled her down lanes of unreadable tombstones behind rusty iron fences, muttering as she went. "It's round here somewhere." Then she stopped short and pointed in triumph.

Barb eyed the brown spire topped with a fat stone urn. "What's so special about that?"

"Read it."

Barb read:

In memory of
EMILY LYDIA
MATHER
beloved daughter of
JOHN & DOVE MATHER
OF RAINHILL, ENGLAND.
MURDERED 24th DEC^R 1891,
AT WINDSOR, MELBOURNE,
AGED 26 YEARS.
Erected by public subscription.

"Christmas eve, hey?" she said. "Emily missed out on the pudding then?"

"Yeah, but cop the next bit," said Leith happily and she started to read out the poems on the base of the monument.

WHO ALL HER DAYS WHILE YET ALIVE
TO LIVE IN HONOUR SHE DID STRIVE.
TILL HE SHE TRUSTED AS HER GUIDE
WITHOUT CAUSE OR WARNING
HER LIFE DENIED.

She shone among the faded grass, delighted by her discovery. Barb liked the way Leith was clever and different, but for some reason her mouth had stopped smiling. She turned and looked out of the cemetery, across all the suburbs crowding in a pink blur to the blue-grey hills beyond.

"I don't get it."

"Her hubby killed her," Leith explained gleefully, and began rolling out the next poem.

ADVICE
TO THOSE WHO HEREAFTER COME REFLECTING
UPON THIS TEXT OF HER SAD ENDING;
TO WARN HER SEX OF THEIR INTENDING,
FOR MARRYING IN HASTE, IS DEPENDING
ON SUCH A FATE, TOO LATE FOR AMENDING.

Barb could see the bare boards, the bundle of old-fashioned clothes fallen in a heap to the floor, the man who turned away studying big fine hands like Claudio's hands. And Leith was dancing in front of the grave.

"Isn't it the worst poetry you ever heard? Great, hey?"

"No," said Barb, and walked off. Six steps away, she couldn't remember what it was all about. She stopped, and Leith trailed up like a giant spaniel.

"Sorry, but—um. She's dead, after all."

Now Leith would get upset and the whole thing would really go out of control. But no, Leith just considered for a moment and said, "Yeah, you got a point. But I still reckon the poems are a hoot."

So there she was, behaving like Leith; with Leith being the sensible one.

Normally Barb slept in on Sundays, but for once she was up early, the books for her history test spread across the desk, and last night replaying itself whenever she gave it the chance.

First: the car by the park, lights tracking the road, the grass as black as a bottomless lake, and Barb staring out the car window at all of it.

"Sorry, I'm just not in the mood."

"No probs."

Next: gentle cuddling, a bit of soft kissing.

"Y'know, Barb, you mean a lot. I've never met a girl like you before. Never felt like saying that 'I love you' stuff before."

Then: Barb sitting there calmly. Claudio saying a whole lot more.

Would he have gone that far if I'd looked keener? The big joke is, I wasn't trying to lead him on this time. I was keeping my mouth shut because I didn't know what to say.

Later: outside Barb's house, urgent gripping hands. "You're driving me crazy, you know that." Unspoken words coming across just as clearly. "You've got to make up your mind soon."

Barb slammed her pen down. "All right, I know I do," she said out loud, and escaped to the house for a cup of coffee. Sue grabbed her in the doorway.

"Barry just rang," she breathed. "He's coming to lunch."

Good for Mum — and good for me to stop brooding, thought Barb, as the house went into high speed round Mrs O'Connell. Sue picked flowers; Mrs Hartwell made a Yorkshire pudding; Barb read the end of a local history Barry had lent her, while she chopped the vegetables.

When Barry arrived, Mrs O'Connell accepted a kiss on her carefully powdered cheek and handed him over to her family as a special treat.

Everything worked in Barry's favour. If his black hair was receding, it showed off a round, serious forehead. His slight paunch filled tailored slacks with a solid dignity. He had something for everyone, swinging Sue off her feet, sniffing the air for the roast, bringing out a huge box of chocolates, and a smaller box for Mrs O'Connell.

"Barry. You shouldn't." As she fitted the two demure pearls in her ears, her face softened behind the make-up. "How do I look?"

"Lovely," said Barry at once, "and the pearls are nice too," with a wink at the others.

Over lunch he argued with Barb and Mr Hartwell about the elections, proving with his accountant's logic that Mr Hartwell, being self-employed, would be better off under the Liberals.

Mr Hartwell sniffed, "Always voted Labor, and always will," and Barb got stuck into the Liberals' policies on unemployment. Sue wriggled with boredom, her mum smiled encouragingly, and Barry explained how the Liberals' economic programme would create more jobs in the long run.

"So if I can't get a job when I leave school, like heaps of kids now, I'm supposed to think, 'At least some businessman's getting richer'?"

"No, of course that's not good enough," said Barry warmly. "I don't feel I'm let off the hook just by voting. I give a lot of support to my church's drop-in centre for unemployed youth, for example." He smiled. "Not that you need to worry, Barb. With your marks you should get into teachers college easily — and if not, there's always a place for a bright young junior in my office."

Barb frowned her way back to her history books. The fact was, she had been deliberately stirring Barry, and all he had done was offer her a job. But what if he hadn't made it up with Mum? Would she still have been a bright young junior, no strings attached?

Monday morning felt the way it was supposed to: lousy. Leith cornered her in the foyer and babbled away about someone called Emily Lydia Mather, and Barb gave her a blank, sleepless stare.

"I'll tell you later, then," Leith said sadly, and let Trina and Pam sweep her away.

Barb was waiting for the history teacher and the history test when it sank in: Leith had gone to the city library and read up on the murdered woman, all because Barb had said it was more than a joke. Her smile was spreading through her whole body when Cass Rosenbloom leaned across to ask, "You watching *The Edwardians* tonight?"

"That new BBC series? What are Edwardians, anyway?"

"King Edward, ya dodo, like Elizabethans for Elizabeth I. He came after Queen Victoria, so that's sort of 1900, but I think the Edwardian age covers the 1890s too, maybe 'cause Victoria was old and out of it."

"Hey, that makes Leith's tombstone Edwardian — if it applies to Australia as well as England."

"Leith's tombstone? What are ya?"

Telling Cass about Emily Lydia Mather was like double-underlining the fact that her opinions mattered to Leith. And Cass liked the story. Mr Richmond had to cough three times before she would stop asking Barb questions, and after class she dragged Barb off to tell the whole thing to Mark Douglas.

But Barb had planned this one. "You ought to ask Leith Dunbar. She knows stacks more than me."

Mark nodded. "I want some stuff about Melbourne in the past for the magazine, see? Tell Leith to come and talk to me at lunchtime."

Leith had started out slowly, but now she was really into it. "So I looked at all the newspapers for the 24th of December, 1891 — and there was nothing about the murder in any of them."

"A hoax tombstone," breathed Cass, rapt.

Mark looked scornful. "Come on, you don't send a notice to the papers to announce you've murdered someone. Did you look at the next day, Leith?"

"And the next, and the next," agreed Leith. "I read weeks of musty old newspapers and then, just as the library was closing, I saw these headlines."

"Well?" demanded Xenia.

"He'd buried her under the hearthstone in front of the fireplace, so no-one would find her." Leith dropped her voice. "But the body swelled as it decayed, and forced up the hearthstone, and people realised—"

"By the smell," Paul muttered ghoulishly, and Cass pushed him.

"Yuck. Stop it."

"It's like she was trying to get out and go after him." Xenia's black eyes glittered. "It'd make a great play. Or, hang on, we could dress up as—what was it?—Edwardians, and lay a wreath on her grave, the day she died."

"Save your acting for the youth theatre," advised Mark. "You don't have to get into period gear to lay a bloody wreath, you know."

"Well, we could do something else; tie it in with *The Edwardians* on the box," said Xenia readily. "What else do Edwardians do?"

"In the novels they're always going boating. You could go rowing on the river."

Xenia thought for a moment. "Yea, I can see it. Saturday arvo on the Yarra, all the happy families on their outings, and zap!" Her long hands wove patterns on the air. "Suddenly they're faced with these ghosts from the past, kind of refugees from *Picnic at Hanging Rock*. We'd freak 'em out of their tiny skulls. Leith can read up on it and tell us what to do. What d'you reckon, team?"

"I like it." Cass bounced and her earrings, coils of pink and green plastic, bobbed wildly. "Come on, Mark, you're supposed to be into Melbourne history. Here's your chance to see how it really felt."

Barb looked at Mark too, willing him to say it was all garbage. She had just come along in support of Leith, not to get dragged into one of the great Xenia Anastasiou Show-off Schemes. She barracked under her breath as Mark shrugged impatiently and Paul mumbled, "Maybe Leith doesn't want to take on bulk reading, just so we can pretend we're Edwardians."

But Leith was caught in a net of excited looks between Cass and Xenia, saying, "Why not?"

Mark strode off towards Central, leaving Leith to follow slowly and think about writing something for a real magazine. Xenia had to touch her arm before Leith realised she was there.

"Okay," she started in straightaway. "Cass is keen; I'll work on Paul; you'll work on Barb; bloody Mark Douglas is as keen as he'll ever be about someone else's idea. But it all depends on you basically, Leith. What d'you reckon?"

Leith blinked into the bright face inches from her own. "Sure."

Xenia sighed with pleasure and plans. "I knew you would. And Paul can do the costumes, seeing he's supposed to be good at art. Besides, he needs to get off his bum sometimes."

"You're pretty different for twins." A whole sentence this time, Leith noted.

"Yeah, reckon I was changed at birth. I'm too tall for a Greek girl anyway. Mind you, Paul isn't your typical Greek male either, thank Christ. There's enough in our family already." She stretched her long body up and out, then nipped at Leith's arm again. "Now, what's this about Trina Dunbar and Karen Swallow?"

"Huh?" Back to one-word answers again.

"Are they *really* your best mates? They don't strike me as your type," said Xenia severely, and Leith shrugged.

"Dunno what my type is. Barb's the only person I really talk to."

"Could you talk to me?" Xenia's jet-black eyes probed.

"Probably. But I never see you."

"Yeah, there's always people."

Straightaway there were people again, Paul and Cass waving Xenia to join them. Leith dawdled behind, walking carefully in case the moment spilled over and was lost.

I didn't even think. I just said like that, I could talk to her. And she sounded as if she really wanted to. She said, "It all depends on you."

Swallow was leaning against her locker, pink bubble gum balloon just bursting. "So what did their majesties want?"

Leith explained unwillingly as she fumbled with the afternoon's books and folders.

"What a batty idea," said Swallow in her most rasping voice. "When's it on? This I got to see!"

It was too easy to imagine Swallow, hands in pockets, lounging by the river and taking it all in. Leith turned with a pleading look, and Swallow grinned maliciously and teased her for the date all the way to class.

After school Leith raced to the library and gathered up a pile of books about the Edwardians. Then suddenly she didn't believe it had happened. She would do all the work and Xenia would just stare— "Jesus, you didn't think I meant it?"

She weighed the books in her arm for a moment, then reached for the borrowing forms. After all, it wouldn't hurt to know more about the Edwardians.

All that night, finding facts in the books and printing them neatly onto file cards, Leith hummed with happiness. Edwardian women wore huge hats covered with wax fruit and stuffed birds. Table napkins were folded into shapes, each with a name—the Fleur de Lis, the Rose and Star, the Sachet, the Slipper. And at breakfast in the country houses, silver dishes on the sideboard, warmed by little blue flames, held eggs and bacon, kedgeree, haddock, sausages, kidneys, porridge with thick yellow cream.

It was another world and, file card by file card, Leith escaped into it.

6
CHOOSING TO CHOOSE

Paul Anastasiou came wandering down the corridor, his old coat flapping around him. Leith had been dodging him and his lot for two days now, scuttling out of class on Miss Vincini's heels, copping it from Pam for refusing to hang round Dungeons and Dragons.

Now she turned her back and pretended to read a noticeboard. *If it's all off, I don't want to know. If Xenia doesn't want to be my friend, I don't want to know.*

She looked round cautiously to find Paul and Xenia right behind her.

"You're bloody hard to pin down," accused Xenia. "Have you done any work yet? Can you come to the op shops with us after school, Friday?" Leith nodded dumbly. "Good," Xenia approved. "Go on, ask her, Paul."

Leith had to get him to repeat his mumbles twice, then she had to gasp more air into her lungs. "Join Dungeons and Dragons? Me?"

"Who else?" snapped Xenia. "Well, yes or no?"

Paul rolled his eyes. "Feel free to think about it. She gets off on bossing people around."

I can't—I've got to—if I don't . . . Out of a flurry of half-finished thoughts Leith said, "Yes," and Xenia gave a satisfied smile.

"See?" she said to Paul. "This one's the careful sort—you have to twist her arm. Lunchtime then."

Leith could feel her feet floating free from the ground. Then she was being tugged back by an accusing circle of Trina, Swallow and Pam. *I've had lunch with you for four years, you can't complain,* she told Trina and Swallow. But still she felt heavier and heavier, till she remembered that Xenia had bothered to notice that she was the careful sort.

"What d'you do when you have to choose, but you'd rather do both things?"

Mr Dunbar cracked his knuckles thoughtfully. "It depends on what you mean by 'have to'. If you have to choose between two films, you can see one now and the other later. If you have to choose between two TV programmes, you have to choose absolutely. Or hire a video recorder," he added.

Leith sliced extra hard at the carrots and wished her father would save his logic for his philosophy students at uni. "No, I mean if *people* are making you choose between them," she insisted.

"Can they really make you choose?"

"Well, they can say, 'Either you're friends with us, or you're friends with them.'"

In actual fact, Trina had sniffed and gone on with her maths, Pam had scowled, and Swallow had said airily, "Go right ahead— but don't forget to take a clean hanky," leaving Leith with the uncomfortable feeling that for some reason she had been asking their permission.

"But you can still look for other options," Mr Dunbar was saying. "You can go on trying to be friends with both groups, for example."

I did try, Leith argued to herself. I went and talked to them, and they didn't say anything then, and after school in the corridor Trina and Pam—they walked right past me, as if I wasn't there.

"Sure," she told her father. "I can still only have lunch with one lot."

"That's true—on any given day. But you could have lunch with one group one day, the other the next. Or you could see one group at recess and the other at lunchtime. There's all kinds of possibilities," said Mr Dunbar cheerfully, tipping onions into the pan.

Leith whanged her knife onto the last carrot. It sounded like her father was taking Swallow and Trina and Pam's side against her. Well, Barb was pleased, anyway.

On Friday they all ended up in the Anastasious' kitchen. It shone clean—fresh mauve and aqua paint with a brilliant white trim, cupboards glossy with wiping, a stiff tablecloth displaying a bowl of polished fruit, even a patterned cloth for the toaster.

Mrs Anastasiou smiled and brought honey cakes, pastry twirls topped with sesame seeds and coffee. Leith smiled back and was sorry when Xenia shooed her mother out of the room.

"We've got the clothes, we've got the six pages of stuff Leith typed for us. Now we have to work out our characters," Xenia commanded.

"How about the D & D method?" mumbled Paul.

"What's that?" snapped Barb, straining to hear him, and Cass bustled in to explain about rolling dice to decide how you scored on different character traits.

"Sounds a bit false," said Barb, still determined not to fit in too easily.

Mark shook his head. "It's like how you don't get to choose if you're tall or short, or if your dad's rich or poor." He lolled back on the spindly chair. "Like, I got this really low score for strength once, and it totally changed how I saw myself in the game."

"But this is more of a fantasy than a game," Leith broke in earnestly. "I mean, we'll have the clothes to start us off, but—"

"Hang on, putting on different clothes doesn't mean putting on a different way of behaving," Paul objected.

"Oh yeah?" snapped Xenia. "Try wearing a dress for a day."

They argued for a while, then started inventing characters. Leith kept drifting back to the way they had looked in the op shop—Cass staring in disgust at a tatty bridesmaid's dress, then winding an orange scarf round her waist and adding a long string of purple beads; Mark smoothing out the ruffles on a dinner shirt when he thought no-one was looking; Xenia seizing on dress after dress, then deciding she would go through the wardrobe at the youth theatre.

And in between, came these flashes of Swallow's face as she walked past the group outside Central—totally blank but, for some reason, Leith kept thinking, hurt.

Xenia was prodding her to get her attention. "Cass's mum," she repeated. "We need a comic figure, and you've got all those black clothes, you can be a widow, fussing over Cass and keeping her away from me and Mark, the outrageous types. And Paul can be your brother; he wants to be a sort of eccentric lord."

"And Barb?" asked Paul.

"A maid. We need a maid, and they've definitely got costumes at the youth theatre."

"I thought, something more interesting. A prostitute, maybe," Barb challenged Xenia, but Mark frowned.

"Not for a boat trip, hey, Leith?"

"Sorry, Barb."

"Oh well, looks like I'm stuck with the maid," Barb shrugged, losing interest. "Leith, we got to go if we want to make the shops."

Leith and Mrs Anastasiou smiled their way to the door. "Thanks for the coffee and cakes," said Leith, wondering what it would be like to have a mother around all the time.

"No worries," said Mrs Anastasiou, and her quiet, lined face looked like Xenia's for a moment.

Barb selected shirts, jeans, boots, as speedily as Leith had sorted out facts about the Edwardians.

"Call it 'the Look', if you like," whinged Leith, turning to and fro in a baggy cardigan. "I call it 'the Rip-off'—making you get everything new so it matches. How d'you know all this stuff about what goes with what, anyhow?"

"I just do," said Barb firmly. "Like, magazines, what's in the shops, what people are wearing. You could work it out for yourself, if you really wanted to."

"Maybe." Leith grinned. "Right now I want to eat. We've got enough money left for Chinese."

As the food arrived she was asking about Claudio.

"Yeah, he reckoned he couldn't see me this week," said Barb. "Work stuff, and his sister's going on a trip to Italy. But if you ask me, I'm supposed to realise what I'm missing and decide to get off with him."

"D'you want to?"

"Yeah. Sort of. See, the problem is, if I get off with him once, then I'll have to go on doing it, if you see what I mean."

"No," said Leith frankly. "Do you love him, then?"

Barb carefully separated a mushroom out from the other vegetables. "What I keep thinking is, maybe it's me. Half the kids I know have been getting off with guys for years. Am I scared or something? Not normal?"

She stared at the mushroom, waiting for Leith to pass judgement, but when she finally looked up Leith was goggling at her.

"Half the kids? People I know? Like who?"

"Look, take my word for it, okay?"

Leith kept on gaping, and Barb started to feel better about herself. Leith was probably the original "sweet sixteen and never been kissed" — why was she worrying? And funnily enough, it helped, the way Leith treated the whole thing like a comprehension exercise, puzzling away and finally saying, "But if you don't like it, you don't *have* to do it again." Her logic could be pretty detached and annoying sometimes, but sometimes it was really useful.

Swallow's blank-hurt face followed Leith all the way home. She walked into the lounge room and said, "That stuff I was telling you before about choosing between two groups — what if I really like one group better?"

Mr Dunbar lifted his pointed nose from his book. He looked like an intelligent bird under his crest of grey hair. "Then you're choosing to choose."

"But I don't want the others to feel bad."

"Why not?"

"What d'you mean?" Leith made a face. "No-one wants to hurt other people."

"Perhaps not, but people get hurt all the same. Why shouldn't they be allowed to feel hurt?"

Her father stared at the night outside in the courtyard, off on his private thoughts, and Leith, left to herself, admitted that the idea was, if Swallow and the others didn't feel bad, then she didn't have to feel guilty. She decided not to open up the whole question of guilt to her father's logic: it would be simpler to ask Trina over, feed Pam some juicy gossip about Mark and see if Swallow wanted to go to a film.

"So do I get to see this stunning new outfit Barb talked us into?" asked Mr Dunbar, stirring himself into cheerfulness.

Leith bounded up the stairs. *Yes. That was the right thing to do. Make the first move.* Harder than hiding away and bitching to herself, but if her father was right and she was making choices, then she had to follow them through.

By the top of the stairs she felt kilos lighter. She stripped and reached for the Myers bag, then changed her mind and scrambled into her Edwardian clothes. Swirling the black skirt around, smoothing the sleek black velvet of the coat, Leith looked into the mirror and saw a woman of grace and confidence.

Hey, remember you're the comic bossy mum, she reminded herself, and quickly changed into Barb's clothes.

Loose lilac shirt, tight black jeans, grey ankle boots, huge cardigan. They did fit together in some mysterious way. She took a step towards the mirror and the boots even made her walk differently. *Hi, party girl.*

Why now, after resisting Barb all this time? wondered Leith as she trod carefully down the stairs. Okay, Barb had been low, it had cheered her up. But they could have seen a movie instead. Leith pushed open the lounge room door, thinking, oh well, I don't have to wear them if I don't want to.

7
JUST YOU AND ME
AND THE DOUBLE BED

Barb was away with flu, and Leith had to face biology on her own. She had worked out a routine which meant that the sports teachers left her alone, but Mrs Simons was harder to con. So Leith worked reluctantly through the experiment, waiting for something to go drastically wrong, and in between she eavesdropped on Con and Gavin at the next bench.

Gavin was pushing, snatching and griping his way through the experiment. "What's up?" Con asked finally.

"What's up, y'self?" But Gavin was still staring at the empty space between his hands, as if he hadn't noticed Con grabbing the glass bottle back from him. Con shook his head.

"Must be all the study, Gav, it's getting to you. You need a night at the pub, checking out the talent. Those young chicks get bigger and better every week."

Leith pulled her mouth down as Con drew it on the air, then gave a second surprised look as Gavin groaned.

Con looked concerned too. "Hey, you crook or something?"

"Feel like I'm crook? Does it?"

All of a sudden Gavin had a headlock on Con. Leith stepped back to protect her experiment, but Con stayed still, gasping, "Feels like you're in a bloody bad mood. Lay off," and Mrs Simons swooped down to give Gavin her brief, edited opinion of him.

Things went quiet for a while then, and Leith was actually getting interested in her work when she heard Gavin say more calmly, "Con, how come we always hang around with younger chicks?"

"'Cause chicks our own age see us in class every day. They'd never think we were that big deal!"

Dead right, agreed Leith silently. She sneaked a look at Gavin, washing his hands at the sink, slow and steady, with a sunken unhappy look on his broad, freckled face. So what was that all about? wondered Leith, and forgot it for the next few days.

Back at school again, Barb decided she had better test out on Silvana and Debbie the idea of wearing fancy dress in public.

"Oh yeah, who's the big attraction — Paul or Mark?" teased Debbie.

"Come on, Deb, she couldn't be interested in Paul — that daggy coat, and looking like he hasn't eaten since he was twelve."

"Ah, he's all right.'

"Gotcha!" crowed Debbie. "Your Eytie wonder better watch himself, there's some real competition on the scene now."

"You don't really like Paul Anastasiou better than Claudio?" asked Silvana wide-eyed.

"Get away. I said he was all right, not I'm going to marry him."

"So how's things with you and Claudio, anyhow? What's he like?" Debbie leered.

"You're a sex maniac."

"Best kind to be."

Barb was starting to drop a few hints about sex with Claudio when she found she was blushing. The harder she tried to stop it, the redder her cheeks got.

"Haven't you done it with Claudio yet?" Debbie gaped, but Silvana just nodded and went on, "Makes sense if you're serious about him. Whatever they say, most Italian guys respect a girl who keeps them waiting."

Debbie started to speak, looked round and dropped her voice. "D'you mean you're a *virgin*?"

Barb fiddled with her scarf. "You make it sound like something in a science fiction movie."

Silvana said helpfully, "I didn't want to either, not till I met Craig," and Debbie turned the stare onto her.

"Hang about, I thought you and Angelo were having it off years ago."

"Yeah, well. We *nearly* did."

Debbie took a long hard look at both of them. "True confession time." She stood up and tugged her skirt into place on her plump hips. "What's so big deal about the whole thing, anyway? Come on, the siren's gone."

I'm losing my grip, thought Barb in a panic. I've always covered up about me and guys before, it's getting to me. "So what d'you reckon I should do?" she asked quickly, figuring she might as well make the most of it, now they knew.

"Wait till it feels right," said Silvana. "I'm glad it was Craig."

"Let 'er rip," said Debbie. "Forget all that love stuff, it's just good dirty fun."

"Thanks a lot," said Barb sarcastically. "You just solved all my problems."

Leith was casually checking to see if Xenia and the others were still around when Barb pelted out of Central, grabbed her by the arm and pushed her off down the street.

"What's the rush?"

"Jesus, it was amazing." Barb was pink with giggles. "You'll never guess, not in a million years."

"So tell me."

"Gavin Petty comes up to me at the lockers, right? He ums and ahs and shuffles round, then he goes, 'Do you want to go out with me some time?'" Barb's eyes glittered. "Gavin Petty!"

"What did you say?"

"What d'you reckon? I went, 'Oh, I always see my boyfriend at the weekend,' and he went, 'Well, that's that, I s'pose.' And then—get this—Con Theostratis sticks his head round the corner to see how his best mate's making out. Blech!"

Leith could hear Con's voice again. "Chicks our age would never think we were that big deal." Gavin's sad freckled face. She said, "Wonder how it feels, asking someone out and them saying no."

"Come off it, Leith. Don't expect me to feel sorry for him. He's a fool. He's never even talked to me hardly."

"It'd have to be better than waiting to be asked," Leith went on, and Barb shook her head to and fro.

"But you don't just wait, Leith. There's lots of ways of showing you're ready to be asked. Believe me, that's better than having to lay it on the line."

"I'd rather lay it on the line," said Leith stubbornly.

"So you say." Barb was tempted to add, "Miss Sweet-sixteen-and-never-been-kissed," to punish Leith for spoiling a good story. Still, she could tell Deb and Silv tomorrow, they'd think it was a hoot. Gavin Petty, of all people.

Two-colour tights, Silvana's best shoes, Debbie's off-the-shoulder dress with her huge green leather belt and a really artistic make-up job, seeing they were going to a restaurant instead of the dark old pub.

Barb checked herself over in the mirror for the tenth time. This time she thought she looked twenty-five, which was reassuring; last time she had looked twelve.

"Are you sure?"

Barb didn't want to know whether her mum was worrying about her hair or her hemline this time. She snapped back, "I told you, this is what everyone's wearing," and glared. A good row might take her mind off things.

"I just wanted to ask, are you sure you wouldn't like to take Nan's old handbag?"

And the bag, dripping with beads, was just right. Barb hastily stuffed things into it, while Mrs O'Connell went on cautiously, "Don't worry so much, Barb. Restaurants aren't all that frightening."

It's not the restaurant, thought Barb, it's what happens afterwards. Like, it's not my birthday or his, and neither of us has won Tatts, so what are we celebrating? As if I couldn't guess.

The doorbell rang. Filling the front door, Claudio was all the maniacs from the horror movies at the drive in. Opening the car door he was all the strange men she'd been warned not to accept lifts from.

Then he said, "Hi, my name's Claudio Fantucci." Barb giggled with relief. "You looked so fantastic, see, I thought I'd got the wrong girl."

"So have you?"

"This one'll do me."

Out of the candle-lit shadows of the restaurant gleamed dozens of thirty-year-old women with designer hair, magazine clothes and suave escorts. Claudio just stood there, and Barb had a sudden fear that he wouldn't know what to do either, but a waiter came and led them to a table. Barb sighed with relief and opened a menu.

"Jesus, can you afford this?" she squeaked, and felt uncool again.

Claudio grinned. "Listen, I'm a working man, only a car to support. Besides, I decide what I can afford, so pick whatever you want. How about the lobster?"

"No, I—"

"Come on, lash out."

"I get sick from seafood."

"Oh well, that'd never do." He gave her a long look across the haze of candlelight, and her body stirred again inside the clothes.

The food made patterns on the plate like a flower arrangement, and the steak was soft as watermelon. They swapped tastes, holding their forks out boldly across the heavy red tablecloth, and grinned when the other diners flicked elegant eyes across them.

We've never spent this long just talking before, Barb realised as they waited for the gelati. No band, no movie, no TV, no video games—just me and Claudio. She looked round for something to say.

"D'you reckon that guy's with his wife or his daughter?"

"Dunno. Why?"

"It's just interesting sometimes, guessing about people."

"But you never know if you were right, so it doesn't get you anywhere." Claudio shifted in his seat, then brightened up. "Hey, did I tell you the latest on the new head of our section? That guy has to be the biggest walking disaster area in the public service."

Barb listened and nodded. She couldn't follow half of what he was talking about, but at least it passed the time till the gelati arrived. Since Claudio had been talking about his work, she hoped she could give him a run-down of the end of term tests, but she soon realised it wasn't on and skidded to a halt.

"Jeez, I'm glad I'm out of all that," said Claudio as Barb quickly dug into the sparkling crumbs of ice. "I couldn't wait to leave school, only stuck it out so's I'd get a decent job."

"Weren't you scared you still mightn't get a job?"

"Not me, baby, I'm not one of those bludgers."

"Hang on, Craig took ages to get a job. You can't call him a bludger."

"Fair enough. But I bet he didn't plan ahead. I decided what I was going to do when I was fourteen, then I went for it. That's the way I always work."

Another long look, but Barb almost missed it, too busy with the idea of planning since you were fourteen. She hurried to catch up with what Claudio was saying.

"So that's the deal, my sister and her husband in Italy, and me keeping an eye on their flat. Do us a favour and have coffee there? I can't cook to save my life, but I make a mean espresso."

Just you and me and the double bed. "Why not?"

And it was a breeze. They sat on the couch drinking coffee and telling each other what a great evening they had had.

"You really can make coffee."

"Anything for you. Honest." His opal eyes looked right into hers. "Y'know, I've been out with chicks who—you take them somewhere, and all the time they're putting down the waiter and that, trying to show you it's no big deal to them. But with you, it's like you're so at ease with yourself, you make other people feel that way too."

Great, that's what you're supposed to think. She smiled dreamily, and Claudio reached for her.

Kissing, cuddling, hands sliding here and there. Barb felt warm and boneless. She mumbled a protest as Claudio sat up, smoothing his hair, and asked, "More coffee?"

"Not for me."

"Hey, I should've said before, d'you want to have a look round the flat? It's a great place."

And there's only one room I can't see from here. What the hell, why not?

Lazy and peaceful, she followed Claudio to the bedroom, where she dawdled over the silver-framed photos on the dressing table till he said, "Come here."

He was lounging on the bed, shoes off, coat hanging on the ornamental bedside chair. Barb kicked off her own shoes and joined him.

"You're a long way off," Claudio teased, and it did make the tidy room more friendly when she snuggled against him, though the family photos still embarrassed her a bit when Claudio started to slide the dress even further off her shoulders.

The wine at dinner helped. The bed helped—no way would Barb have gone this far in the back of a car, with perves or cops likely to peer in at any minute. It helped that Claudio had taken her to such a posh joint—he didn't think she was easy. And for a while Barb just enjoyed the new feeling of skin sliding on skin, while the planning part of her mind tried to remember how Claudio had managed to undress her so efficiently.

Then he swung away from her, unfastening his trousers. The air fingered coldly into every part of her nakedness. Barb started to curl up.

"No, let me look at you. God, that's beautiful."

His trousers dropped to the floor. Barb remembered gratefully that *Girl* said women weren't interested in looking so she concentrated on Claudio's face, intent, dreamy, staring so hard he was almost looking through her. Stretched out on the bed in a circle of light, Barb all at once felt very lonely.

"D'you really want to?" *Why not?* "D'you use anything?"

"Huh? No," said Barb indignantly when she worked out what he meant.

"Don't worry, I'll take care of you." Claudio clicked the bedside lamp off. "So I'm the first," he said in the darkness as he pressed down on her again.

Barb had a very clear picture of running, out the door, down the stairs, into the street. Her heart was battering her ribs, but she hadn't moved, she was still here in a strange flat on a strange bed.

"Relax. It won't hurt if you relax."

After all, you couldn't run out into the street naked, Barb reasoned. So she ran the film again. Just grab for the dress and the bag, slam the door, pull on the dress, hail a taxi, get Mum to pay if it's too much—and tell her what? See? She had to go through with it.

"Are you ready?"

How would I know?

I don't exist. This is happening to someone else.

"Give us a go, Barb," panted Claudio. "You said you were ready, we've got to, now."

Everyone does it. Deb, Silv, Mum, Nan, everyone . . . Barb clenched herself against pain, relaxed, tightened; and as Claudio pressed forward again she jerked herself as far away as possible from a second pain, squeezing her legs shut.

Bodies scuffled, arms and legs struck against each other, hair tugged. Claudio's hips ground to a slow halt and she lay bruised under his heavy body and heavier breathing, her thighs damp, her heart slowing to a funeral march.

The next few seconds were the longest in her life so far. Her wide-open eyes watched the grey streetlight seep in through the bars of the venetian blinds, picking out the white blob of a bride in the dressing table photos. Her left breast lolled sideways like a leaking balloon under Claudio's forearm, which was all cobwebbed with black hair. Barb was counting the doorknobs on the built-in cupboards when he said dully, "You shouldn't have done that."

"I'm sorry," said Barb's voice.

"Well, you're still a virgin. Since that seems to be so important. Reckon it's made of stainless steel."

The words echoed in the grey room. "I said I'm sorry."

"Ah, yeah, that makes it all terrific, doesn't it?"

Claudio flung himself away. His clothes rustled in the silence.

Barb stumbled up and fumbled with zips and hooks and buttons, slowing when she realised she'd soon have to turn and face him. Then the door thudded behind him and she had a few minutes to brush her hair, look helplessly at the mirror.

Claudio was waiting for her. He looked like a TV actor, his hair smoothed into its handsome thickness, his lines prepared.

"You weren't to know, I s'pose," he said formally. "Come on, I'll drive you home."

For a while Barb could only remember that she had left the bed unmade, tossed and crumpled in the middle of that neat flat. Then she figured that Claudio would go back sometime and change the sheets. After that she tried to think of words to reach across the gap between them, but she could only hear one.

Failed.

She could smile or joke or flirt or look cool, and she would only make a bigger fool of herself. She'd spoiled it for Claudio, and she'd spoiled it for herself. *Failed, failed.*

The car stopped.

"See you. Thanks for the dinner. It was great."

"Sure. Give you a ring some time."

Barb's hands had unfastened the seat belt and were closing round the door handle when she knew she didn't want it to end like this. And she was leaning over at a crazy angle, pushing a kiss against Claudio's jaw. He went on staring ahead through the windscreen.

So she was out of the car and rattling her key in the lock, still thinking, It can't end like this. The rev of the engine thundered in her ears, and she turned to see the car halfway down the street. Barb let herself in and went down to the lounge.

Barry and her mum were sitting at opposite ends of the couch. A great night all round, Barb noted. She mumbled a quick hello and ducked into the bathroom, where she pulled off her clothes with shaking hands and stepped under the shower.

The water beat down, washing away the smells and touches of the night, swirling them round her feet, gurgling them down the drain. Barb towelled herself briskly and made for the bungalow, though she couldn't help seeing Mrs O'Connell whisk a tissue away from her eyes as she passed.

She hung up Deb's dress, slid herself between stiff clean sheets and clenched her whole body to keep from howling for Mum. I'll give her some kind of story in the morning, Barb thought sensibly. Then her mind unlocked, releasing quick flashes of memory, and she started to cry, soft splashing tears that went on and on, washing the memories away again, floating her into sleep.

And then she was fighting wildly, pushing to get free, shouting, "Daddy. Daddy."

Barb's face worked with tears. She was choking. Under her hands was wool, the blanket, and once she realised that, she was able to sit up, stare at the silver cups gleaming in the nightlight.

I dreamed I was in our old house and Dad was sick and we all walked past and didn't see him.

She was in the bungalow. But crying like she'd cried two years ago, when they said, "Come into the front room," which was for visitors, and then said, "Barb, Sue, there's something we have to tell you."

Oh God, thought Barb. I thought I'd got over the nightmares. They're so pointless. He went off to Moya, and Mum's better off, and I didn't even really like him. There's nothing to be sad about.

She lit one of her rare cigarettes. At the third puff she told herself plainly that Claudio wouldn't ring, she would never see him again. At the fourth puff she told herself plainly that she'd failed.

She had really liked Claudio, but she couldn't get off with him. She must be frigid or a lesbian or something. Not normal. In a word, stuffed. Forget about "pretty and clever and good fun"—from here on, it was Gavin Petty or nothing, which meant nothing.

A jingle kept running through her mind, over and over. "Till he she trusted as her guide/Without cause or warning her life denied." She couldn't go to sleep till she remembered that it came from Leith's tombstone.

8
ROWING DOWN THE RIVER

Cass, in her ragged bridesmaid's dress jazzed up by purple beads and orange sash, fluttered her eyelashes at Mark. Paul peered at them over a huge false moustache. Xenia, in a tight red dress and black cartwheel hat, poised on Mark's arm. While Leith held up her great-grandmother's lorgnette and waited miserably for the photographer to finish.

Why did Xenia have to go and ring up the local paper? They were all wrong — Cass's hair stiff with gel and striped purple for the day; Mark's jeans; Paul still wearing that daggy old coat over his tweed suit. At least Xenia's clothes from the youth theatre were historical — but from the 1930s, not the 1890s.

Leith had tried so hard to get everything just right — sewing lace mittens, pinning artificial roses on her hat, fixing buckles to her shoes, borrowing an old shawl and jewellery from her grandmother, dreaming about the Edwardians constantly.

And here she was, the odd one out as usual. It was even worse when you didn't fit in *because* you'd got everything right. Leith made her face stiff as the photographer lined up one last shot, then stiffened even more as a woman in a fashion tracksuit surged forward, pushing her friend ahead of her.

"Take a closer look at the girl with the eyeglasses on the little gold stick. That's a lorgnette, Cora. Great-aunt Anne used one till her dying day."

The friend mumbled indistinctly.

"Oh, stare all you like," screeched the tracksuit woman. "That's what they're doing it for."

Just as Leith was about to crumple completely, Cass grabbed her hand.

"Where's Barb? Should we ring her?"

Xenia scowled across, and Leith slowly remembered that she

was Dame Leith Dunbar today, and Barb was her maid.

"My dear Cassandra, it's hardly our place to go running around after the servants," she said, studying Cass through the lorgnette.

Cass's eyes popped open, then she remembered too. "Yes, Mama," she said with a grin.

Xenia nodded approvingly, and Leith decided she might be looking forward to the rest of the day, after all.

Barb just shrugged when she heard she had missed the chance of her photo in the paper. On four hours' sleep her eyes were gritty, her ears sang and the ground kept dropping away, then zooming back with a jolt. Luckily being a maid meant standing back while Leith and Cass and Xenia talked nonsense together.

Then Paul waved them down to the rowing boat, and Xenia tossed over her shoulder, "Picnic basket, O'Connell."

I'm not her bloody servant, thought Barb indignantly; then she remembered that she was, for today. As she bent down to pick up the basket, her groin twinged with last night's pain, and the sunlight dimmed into the grey chill of Claudio's sister's flat.

What am I doing here, playing stupid kids' games?

Barb could have sat down and cried for her and Claudio all over again. But she took hold of the picnic basket and forced herself, step by step, back to the laughing group.

The boat rounded a bend in the river and they left cars and kiosks and tracksuits behind. The air hummed with insects, trees piled up to a smooth blue sky and the sun bubbled through the water behind the oars. Cass opened a coloured umbrella and Xenia demanded her turn at the oars.

"Sexist bastard," she snapped when Mark objected.

"Give us a go. Even if you're supposed to be the liberated type, you'd still take it for granted that the blokes would row. Right, Leith?"

" 'Fraid so."

Xenia scowled again, and Cass said quickly, "We're getting out of character . . . Mama, can I have a red suit like Countess Xenia?"

"Certainly not," rapped Leith. "Red, indeed. People would say you were fast."

"Fast," breathed Cass, impressed, and they started making up scandalous gossip, Edwardian style, about people at Central.

"Some say that Signora Vincini comes from an old Italian family—but others say she's only in her thirties."

What was I complaining about before? wondered Leith. Who were the Edwardians anyway? Carefree people, living before the world wars, enjoying the luxury of the moment. Like us now.

She counted them up: kind, friendly Cass; thoughtful Paul; Mark with his muscled arms, gold-furred as he strained at the oars; Xenia the dragonfly darting and flashing all over the place. Leith loved them all.

Happiness was a pain between her breasts. She leaned forward to ease it, trailing her fingers in the warm honey water, while the voices went on making patterns about her. It *is* possible, Leith promised herself. Friends who talk and share ideas. Players for this game of lace and drapery and sunshine, no-one else around and river sounds, this real dream world.

With every minute Barb felt more left out. She hated Xenia for landing her with this lousy maid business. She hated Leith for stepping into the centre of attention. Most of all she hated herself. Silent at the back of the boat, she had plenty of time to build up more proof that she was frigid or a lesbian, and she used every minute.

Then they stopped for afternoon tea, and suddenly Barb was in the thick of things—juggling cups and thermoses of tea, plastering endless scones with jam and cream, passing the sugar, passing the milk, taking orders.

"Another tea, O'Connell," called Cass, and Barb nearly threw it in her face. Part of her knew Cass didn't mean it, she was just playing; but part of her wanted to throw the game in their faces too.

Except that then she would be stuck in a rowing boat with a capital-D Drama. So Barb blocked her ears and slashed at scones, till the boat heaved and the knife was lifted from her hand. By

Paul, who had been mumbling something as he climbed over.

"You've always been a radical, Paul," Leith answered, using her lorgnette. "You can't encourage the lower classes, they'll only take advantage of you."

Paul spread jam neatly and thoughtfully. "There's something I haven't told you, sister Leith," he said. "Barbara and I were married last week in a private ceremony. To you Barbara is one of the lower orders — to me she is part of the wind of change that has to sweep through the decadent upper classes. She and I," his long arm circled Barb's shoulder, "have pledged our lives to the cause of socialism and bloody revolution."

Barb liked it. "Let the ruling classes tremble," she declaimed, from a demo she'd seen in the city sometime. Xenia looked daggers at them both for taking over her game, and Barb thought cheerfully, Sucks to you.

The game went on, but now she was part of it. Dame Leith trembled with shock and horror and dropped her lorgnette. Mark helped with plans for the revolution — the first step being for people to fix their own scones. And as they packed up Leith's picnic basket and rowed back through the late afternoon, they started to return to their ordinary selves and Barb felt totally comfortable again.

"Hope you didn't mind getting married to me all of a sudden," muttered Paul. "Thought you looked a bit left out."

"Yeah, well, you took her way out left instead," punned Mark. "I nearly cracked up, Barb, when you went, 'Let the ruling classes tremble.' Best bit of the day."

Barb laughed with the rest of them, but she had missed her chance to thank Paul. So when Xenia clamoured for coffee and Paul mumbled, "In a false moustache? No way," Barb offered her place. She could feel depressed again afterwards.

Cass and Mark went off, but the other four paraded for Barb's family, then settled down in the backyard for the replay. Xenia stretched out her long legs, red skirt hitched up to make the most of the sun.

"So how d'you reckon it went?"

"It was the most incredible thing that's ever happened to me,"

Leith said without thinking. The others looked startled. "Well, it was," she insisted.

"Mostly due to you," mumbled Paul.

"I second that." Xenia's hand squeezed Leith's lightly, then flew into the air to stress her next point. "And, y'know what? we kept in character for over an hour. Not bad for beginners."

"Beginners? Pretty modest of you, Xeens."

"I didn't mean *me*, I meant the rest of you," Xenia explained, and Paul laughed.

Leith relaxed and listened to the twins' patter, the back of her hand still glowing from Xenia's touch. It was harder to say anything now she wasn't Dame Leith, but she stirred herself when Paul muttered about going home.

"You can get a lift with m'father. What time d'you have to be home?" asked Leith.

"How about three in the morning—really give the old man something to sweat about?"

"Mum sweats too, Xeens, when you pull one of your stunts."

"Tough. Anyone who chooses to live with that bastard deserves to sweat."

The air between the twins tightened. Barb and Leith shifted in their chairs, and Paul turned to explain. "Dad laid into Mum a lot, a few years back, and Xenia still reckons she should have walked out."

"He hit her?" Leith asked, open-eyed.

"Yeah, he bashed her." Xenia glared, and Leith wriggled miserably, looking away down the yard.

"It's not that easy, though," Barb was saying. "Mum had Nan and Grandad to go to, but she's had a pretty rough time all the same."

Paul nodded, and Xenia sneered. "So you reckon it's better to stay and be bashed, huh?"

"Lay off," mumbled Paul, but Barb lifted her chin and said, "You want to twist what I said, go right ahead."

Xenia flung herself restlessly round in her chair and turned on Leith. "Don't suppose anything sordid ever happens to *your* olds."

"My mother's dead," Leith explained. "Killed in a car crash nine years ago. My father was driving, but luckily he was okay."

Instantly Xenia's eyes opened wide, dark and melting. "You poor kid."

Leith liked the look of sympathy, but she didn't feel she deserved it. People always asked about your parents, and the story had worn smooth over the years.

"No, I don't really know how my father felt . . . Sure, he's never looked like marrying again, but he's a pretty private sort of person, doesn't go out much . . . I don't even remember her, see, I was only seven, so I can't say I miss her . . . Look, plenty of people have non-fatal accidents, it was just bad luck."

The usual answers to the usual questions. But her voice quavered slightly between "bad" and "luck", and suddenly she wasn't as smart and clear as usual—Leith Dunbar, the expert on death. For a moment she was scared, then she let herself hear the words that still circled her heart, warm as the river.

You poor kid.

Xenia lifted her arms and announced to the sky, "Well, we're all doing pretty well, considering," and Leith thought the world could stop right there, as they sat round in the leftovers of their Edwardian gear, talking about their lives, finding out more about each other.

Barb had hardly thought about Claudio for hours, then Xenia launched into this story about Jan Leslie at Central.

"Anyway, finally Katie goes, 'Okay', and Jan turns up with this ginormous bunch of roses, and pays for her ticket, and sees her home on the tram, just like a big date in an old movie. Katie said she was packing death in case Jan expected the goodnight kiss on the doorstep too. Leslie by name, and lessie by nature, hey?"

She nudged Leith with a "Lesbie friends", and Leith giggled. Barb was back in the fatal moment when she pushed Claudio away. Her stomach churned.

Lesbian or frigid. Failed. Everyone laughing at me.

She was glad when the others left. Furious when she leapt up to answer the phone during dinner, and it was only Barry.

Tired as death when she lay down in bed and waited for the thoughts to start, and found she didn't care about anything any more, and slept.

9
AT GAVIN PETTY'S PARTY

Leith had Miss Vincini for English too. While she tore strips off everyone about their end of term tests, Swallow gave her usual running commentary and Leith fought her usual losing battle with the giggles. Finally she snorted out loud. Swallow quietly marked another notch on her desk, and Miss Vincini fired off a few short sharp words that kept Leith sober-faced till the end of the lesson.

"Bastard," she said to Swallow as they filed out.

Swallow just grinned. "Well, how was dress-up day, since I kindly didn't come and watch?"

Under those watchful green eyes, Leith kept well away from words like "the most incredible day of my life". Swallow listened in silence, then said briskly, "Very cute. So did you pick up any gossip about your lovely new pals?"

"Not really." Then she remembered the Jan Leslie story. She tried to tell it like Xenia had, but the more she said, the more Swallow screwed up her face like a bulldog.

"Who's spreading that piece of garbage—that pig Douglas?"

"Xenia, actually. Look, can't you lay off them, Swallow?"

"Me? Tell Xenia to lay off Jan, why don't you? Jesus, she makes me spew." Swallow swung away, then glanced back. "Oh, all right. Just don't ask me to be as rapt in them as you are."

From Swallow, that was a gilt-edged apology. "Want to see a film or something in the holidays?" Leith called after her, and Swallow gave the thumbs up sign.

Keeping on with her plans, Leith saw two films with Swallow, talked on the phone to Pam for an hour about Mark and asked Trina and her parents—Mr Dunbar's brother and his wife—to dinner. Then in the last week of the holidays, Paul rang up to see if she was going to Gavin Petty's party.

"No," said Leith definitely. But Xenia grabbed the phone from Paul and in the end she said, "Yes."

As soon as Xenia had hung up, Leith dialled Barb. "Listen, I've never even been to a party. What are you supposed to do?"

"It's not school, Leith, there's no rules. You do what you feel like."

Leith examined this idea for the next few days but it didn't help much. And on the night of the party, when she found herself stranded in a dim passageway with a tape blaring from the end of the house, she basically felt like running. Where had Xenia and Paul vanished to? She took three small steps towards the music, and saw Gavin at the end of the passage.

"Jesus wept, it's Leith Dunbar. Come on in, have a drink, have a joint, have a dance."

Leith thanked Gavin under her breath as she threaded through the dark shapes of people talking, dancing, pashing on against the wall, and found Barb by the mantelpiece. As Barb studied her and adjusted her collar, Leith's breathing started to get back to normal. She looked round, lining up people to stand with if Barb vanished too. Then Con Theostratis jigged out of the crowd and clicked his fingers.

"Go on," said Barb, and gave her a push.

Leith faced Con in total disbelief. For a moment her new grey boots were glued to the carpet, while Con shuffled and swayed opposite her. He jerked his head to say, "Get moving," so Leith twitched her shoulders, lifted her feet and wished she was anywhere else.

Then all of a sudden the music seemed to well up from underneath her. She was dancing, till Con yelled something and she lost it again.

"What?"

"Like this song?"

"Yeah," called Leith, looking right into his face. Wow, she marvelled, me dancing with Con Theostratis, the terror of Central. What next?

The next thing was that Con nodded and strolled off at the end of the track, and Leith turned round to find Barb had gone.

She hovered between two circles of backs, hoping for a space to wedge herself into before someone noticed she was on her own.

Then an aisle opened between the dancers, and she saw Xenia laughing away at the other side of the party. The light outlined her long neck and the overhang of curls, and Leith could fill in the details from memory—the deep creases of her olive eyelids, the soft dark down on her upper lip that had freaked Leith at first, but now seemed part of Xenia's dangerous bravery.

She moved from one foot to the other, wondering if it was okay to barge in on Xenia's group, planning how to make her way casually across the room.

"Leith. It's time we had a dance," said Mark Douglas from beside her.

As soon as Leith had gone off with Con, Gavin came up and asked Barb to dance. It was a bit hard to say no, so she kept a careful distance between them and smiled politely over his shoulder. That should have put him off, but he turned out to be drunk as a skunk, and it seemed safest to race off to the dunny when the track finished.

When she opened the door Gavin was leaning against the door frame. "It's my birthday, I should get a kiss," he explained.

Barb ducked under his arm and said clearly, "I'm not interested, Gav."

"Yeah, but I am."

"It takes two."

Gavin thought about that. "But I like you," he complained. Barb nodded.

"Go and dance with someone else now," she told him. Gavin headed off down the corridor, then came rambling back, forehead creased with the effort of getting his point across.

"I mean it. I like you a lot."

As his arm reached out, Barb side-stepped. "Thanks, mate. Now go on." Gavin thought some more and went. "I'd make a teacher all right," Barb muttered bitterly.

"Not bad," someone agreed behind her. Paul was slouched against the wall.

"You were watching, you creep."

"Sure. Should I have knocked Gav out with a swift uppercut to the jaw, like your noble hubby Lord Paul would've done?"

"Get stuffed. It's just a bit embarrassing." She leaned against the wall next to him, wondering whether to go back to the party or ring for a taxi.

"Want to go for a walk?"

That solved the problem. "Okay," said Barb.

At the end of the rows of sleeping houses a dark stretch of grass opened up. Paul loped onto it, and Barb followed cautiously. "A kids' playground," she discovered, dodging the end of a seesaw.

They sat down on the low-slung swings, the chains cold against Barb's arms as she tipped back and took in the blaze of night overhead. The pulse of single stars, the powdery drift of the Milky Way.

"You really planning to be a teacher?" Paul mumbled. Barb had to ask him to repeat it, then she had to think about it.

"All I'm really good at is studying. So, teachers college," she said in the darkness.

"If you forgot about 'good at', what d'you like?"

"Oh, houses."

She seemed to talk for ages, telling Paul how off most houses were, what you could do instead, how she looked at houses all the time. But then he started talking too, so that was all right — telling her how he wanted to paint, but it was hard to make any money from it. They were working out ways to paint stars when Barb thought, this is crazy. But okay, she decided.

"You're one of the few girls I know who just talks," mumbled Paul into the pause.

"Sexist," said Barb promptly. "Xenia talks. Leith talks. Cass talks. Heaps of girls do." True enough, but she didn't usually go round ticking off guys she didn't know.

"Xenia could talk a bit less," said her twin morosely. "Okay, I admit it, that was a load of bull. I should've said, I like talking to you."

"Great," said Barb, but her voice chilled.

"Don't worry, I'm not about to do a Gavin." He paused and added, "Right at this minute. Um, how'd you feel if I did?"

"A bit weird, at present," said Barb truthfully. Then she felt as if she had to tell him what happened with Claudio. Her breath puffed white against the black and grey shapes of the night as she explained.

"So how did you feel?" asked Paul, interested.

"Lousy. Not normal. Like I must be a leso or frigid or something."

"Yeah, know what you mean. I get it sometimes for liking art — 'What are ya, a poof?' Even asked this guy from the youth theatre — he's homosexual — how he found out about himself." Paul grinned. "He put me in my place. Said it was 'cause he fancied guys."

"Why did that put you in your place? I don't get it."

"Well, I wasn't fancying guys, was I? Hadn't even thought about it." Barb frowned, and Paul tried again. "It was like I was saying: painters aren't real he-men, therefore painters must be poofs, 'cause poofs aren't real he-men. Pretty gross, when you come to think about it."

"But I don't fancy girls," said Barb with an edge to her voice. It sounded like Paul meant that *she* was pretty gross.

"Well then," said Paul peacefully, "why go round thinking you're a leso?"

Barb opened her mouth to tell him why, but she couldn't find the reasons.

"Think you're smart, don't you?" she said crossly.

They swung on the swings, slid down the slides and strolled back to the party in friendly silence. Xenia bounded up to tell them that Leith had pashed on with Mark Douglas for half an hour, then gone off somewhere with him.

"Hope she knows what she's doing," said Barb. Then she did a double-take. "What'm I talking about? Of course she doesn't know what she's doing."

Leith was enjoying herself all the same, cruising through the night streets and thinking about kissing. Like waking up in warm sheets, knowing that something good was happening today, and lying there dreaming about it.

How come I enjoyed it so much when normally I can't stand being touched, she worried. Then she laughed back at herself. No wonder you were careful before, when it has such a big effect on you.

Mark stopped the car and turned to her again. Leith took in the rubbery feel of his tongue for a while. *It's very personal, but it's not what I expected; all wet and slippery, not romantic; not like the books say; nice.* Then she sent her tongue sliding against his as well, and the dreamy feeling got wilder, and they pressed closer, and Leith lost track of the feelings altogether.

Finally Mark pulled away. "That's Johnno's flat," he said thickly, nodding up at a square of yellow light. "Coming in while I collect the booze?"

Warm and cosy and lazy, Leith didn't feel like bright lights and Mark's elder brother.

"I'll stay here," she said, and sat planning the next kiss.

But Mark just dumped the carton of beer in the next seat and drove off straight away. Leith was surprised, then she decided that she didn't really understand how these things worked yet. When Mark pulled up in the middle of nowhere, she turned to him eagerly.

He studied her for a long moment. Then he shook his head. "You're a nice kid. But you don't have a bloody clue what it's all about, and basically I'm not interested in teaching you. So— d'you want to go back to the party, or home?"

"Home, I s'pose," said Leith in a small voice.

Barb rang Leith six times on Sunday, with no luck. So she pounced as soon as Leith walked into the foyer at Central.

"Where were you yesterday?"

"Uncle John organised us all to the Dandenongs, then we had to watch home videos of Trina and the rest for half the night. Boring."

"I was worried."

"Oh. Sorry."

"Well what happened?"

"Nothing much."

The next bunch of kids swarmed in. Leith was elbowed one way, Barb the other. "Tell me in biology," she yelled as she went.

It was clear that she would only get the full story by asking the full list of questions, so she started off with, "What'd he say about Cass?"

Leith repeated, "What?" so loudly that Mrs Simons kept a close eye on them for the rest of the lesson. As they filed out Leith grabbed at Barb's arm.

"Is Mark going with Cass?"

"You must've known. Anyway, it's not your fault, if he made the moves."

"All the same," said Leith darkly, and she went off muttering to herself.

She was more cheerful when they met up after school. "Well, I didn't say a word to Mark all lunchtime — mind you, he didn't say a word to me either. Anyway, then I had a big talk to Cass about the assignment after class. So I think that's all pretty clear now."

"Uh-huh. So Mark didn't turn you on?"

"Oh yeah. I think so."

"You *think* so," Barb repeated scathingly. "Would you have gone the whole way, for example?"

"And get pregnant?" Leith looked shocked.

"Say you were on the pill, then?"

"But I'm not." She considered it. "How would I know? Maybe. It would've been interesting."

"Interesting!" Barb exploded. "Jesus, what are ya?"

After a while Leith asked carefully, "Anything the matter?"

"Nothing big deal. I've only spent all holidays freaking out of my skull cause I couldn't do it with Claudio; and then you have a few lousy kisses and decide sex would be *interesting*."

Leith gave her a gentle questioning look, and Barb started in on the Claudio story again.

Well, fair enough to tell Leith, her friend: but why on earth had she told Paul the other night? She must have been mad, saying all that to a guy. Just the same, when she came to the part about being a leso or frigid, she left out the leso part. It didn't seem to fit any more.

Leith listened, frowning, then said hesitantly, "I don't get it, Barb. I mean, I was packing death Saturday night, just from going to my first party. You're always nervous, the first time." Her face cleared. "So maybe it was his first time too. Maybe he feels bad because he let you down."

"It wasn't his first time," and when Leith still looked doubtful, "Believe me, you can tell."

"Tell me about Mark, then." Leith described the end of her midnight drive, and Barb laughed herself silly.

"Oldest trick in the book. You were s'posed to go up and look at his etchings—get off with him, ya dud. You're lucky he realised you were just ignorant, not a tease."

"See, there *are* rules," Leith muttered sulkily.

Barb rolled her eyes. "There's commonsense, if you know how to use it. So, okay, you were turned on by Mark but you didn't realise he was putting the hard word on you—did you fall for him?"

"I tried to, all Sunday, but," Barb had to move closer to catch the whisper, "I don't think I even like him. It was just sex."

Barb couldn't help laughing again, and Leith looked up with a miserable glare.

"Sorry. I'm not really laughing at you, I was just thinking, wish I had your problems." She could see another question about Claudio on the way, so she said firmly, "Enough of all that garbage. What's been happening to everyone over the holidays?"

Leith launched straight into telling her how Xenia had planned another stunt for the Edwardians. Barb couldn't have been less interested, but Leith insisted on raving on about living history and living theatre and living your dreams and how brilliant Xenia was.

In other words, you've got the hots for her, thought Barb idly. At least, that's what I'd say if Xenia was a guy, she added quickly to herself.

Leith was so innocent. She could easily let herself in for the flak Paul had got for being different, the hell Barb had gone through over the last month, before she talked to Paul. As Leith dragged Xenia's name in for the seventeenth time, Barb shook her head.

"You've got one of your crushes," she warned. "You'd better watch out, or you'll turn into a lesbian."

And she laughed, to make sure it didn't sound too heavy.

10
A DREAM OF XENIA

Over the next few weeks Leith started to say to herself every now and then, I'm a lesbian. She forgot about it in between, but every time she said it, it rang true.

She glanced quickly back over her life to see how it had happened. Crushes on guys in books and films, especially Harrison Ford in *Star Wars*. A big crush on Costa Nikolaides, and then a crush on Trina—both she and Costa were so bright-coloured and bossy and sure of themselves.

Then at Central, Leith had worried heaps about what Barb thought of her. She had been interested in Swallow, but Swallow had clearly liked her, so Leith switched over to Terri Mack who didn't even know she existed. Then Julie Lane, till she left at the end of year 10. And now Xenia.

With Xenia it was different. Not like a game—"If she smiles, it'll be a good day; if not, bad." More like a natural disaster that split Leith's life in two. On one level, her life followed its ordinary patterns of school, home, eat, study, sleep, then the weekend. But underneath, there was this hidden life with its own geography and its own sense of time.

Time flowed when Xenia was around, then dragged itself slowly on till she came again. Leith held a secret map of Central in her head where Xenia's locker and Xenia's form room were her personal sacred sites. She knew that Xenia would stride out of room 201 at 10.00 on Tuesday, and she would walk past in the opposite direction, just to smile and nod. If Xenia wasn't there, she would check carefully, spin around and walk past again.

She memorised Xenia's words and expressions and studied them alone at night. She guiltily stole a few of Xenia's old reserve slips from the library, then hid them away in her desk at home because the sight of the round dashing letters turned her bones to water.

The day Xenia said, "Leith Dunbar's a good listener," she heard nothing but the echoes of the words for hours afterwards.

Loving Xenia turned her life around. In the outside world Leith might still be clumsy or tongue-tied or tactless or different, but underneath she was full of the power of her feelings. Maybe she had nothing to offer Xenia, apart from a few stupid facts about the Edwardians, but at least she could love.

She didn't want to take Xenia to the pictures and give her roses. She didn't even want to be her sidekick—if Xenia lashed out, Leith answered back. Once—after all, she was a lesbian—Leith imagined going to bed with Xenia. She pictured the bed first, then Xenia in it, then a tiny Leith-puppet at the side. Into the bed hopped the Leith-puppet, and straight away it hopped out again.

Leith sighed with relief. She didn't want anything from Xenia. She just wanted her to be there.

Sometimes she tried to work out what it would mean for her future, being a lesbian. Being lonely, of course, separate from other people, a lonely old age. So what else was new? She'd always been lonely. At least this way she had a dream of Xenia for company.

11
INCLUDE ME OUT

Mr Hansen kept Barb back after maths. Since he had started going out with Ms Lee, he had got into this thing of encouraging girl students. Barb didn't mind; she nodded thoughtfully, admired his hollow cheeks and intellectual glasses and tried to trap him into making a guess at how she would go in the exams.

But as she rattled down the stairs her stomach twitched nervously. *Exam panics already? I'll be thin as a rake by November.* Barb shook her head and decided she was just extra hungry. Then she hit the park and saw Debbie laughing away in the middle of Katie Watson's crowd, while Silvana sat by herself at their usual spot. Same as yesterday.

Something's going on, Barb thought. I don't believe Deb is still working on an assignment with Katie. She meant to march over and front up to Deb, but then she took a second look at Silvana and sat down abruptly.

"What's the matter?"

Silvana blinked, her eyes so tender from crying that they even winced at the touch of her eyelashes. "I'm leaving."

"Now? But it's only weeks to the exams. Oh-oh. Are you—?"

"Yeah." Silvana tried to screw her mouth up seriously, but her smile smoothed it out.

"You don't mind, then?"

"There's nothing at school I want to learn. I mean, I don't plan to become a professor, or something, I just want Craig and the baby. So why waste more time?"

"Fair enough. How did your folks take it? You're still in one piece, anyway."

"Just." Silvana blinked again. "It was okay while they were shouting, that's normal. But then they cried. Like, even my dad and my uncle."

"Heavy."

Barb shook her head sympathetically while Silvana sniffed back the tears.

"Ah, I'll survive," she said finally. "I'm staying with my sister while the olds calm down—hey, and she gave me some money to cheer me up. Want to come shopping on Friday night?"

"You can't buy clothes, Silv, they won't fit you in eight weeks."

"You forgot." Silvana giggled. "The baggy look."

"Oh, right," agreed Barb, and she started giggling too. They sprawled on the grass gasping "baggy" at each other for a while, before they sobered up and went on talking about families and babies and flats and Craig.

"Does Deb know?" asked Barb. "S'pose she cleared off to let you tell me."

"Yeah, well." Silvana bit her lip. "Look, I don't know if I'm supposed to tell you, but—Debbie was with Claudio at the pub Friday, and I think he said some stuff to her. About you. So I better warn you, once I'm not around, Deb might—"

"I get the message." Barb's face tightened into a smile. "Thanks, Silv."

Back at school Silvana drifted away in a dream of furniture and recipes and pre-natal classes. She's left Central already really, thought Barb with a chill. I'm on my own now, seeing Deb got to Katie's lot first. Suppose I could always tag along with Leith— except I never let her tag along with me, so it seems a bit unfair.

She pushed the problem to the back of her mind. Too far back, because on Monday she turned up at their usual lunchtime spot again. No Silv. No Deb. It really mattered that Deb didn't see her and have a good laugh, so Barb kept walking briskly till someone stopped her with a hand round her ankle.

"What d'you think you're — oh, Paul," she realised, as he mumbled something about did she want to play cards? Without a second thought Barb sat down at the edge of the group.

She had always thought the Anastasiou crowd probably spent their lunchtimes discussing poetry or something, but they shuffled and dealt and called, and that was that. Barb had plenty of time to feel homesick for Silv and Deb-like-she-used-to-be, before Xenia flung her cards down and announced, "Jesus, this is dead. I've got something I want to talk about."

It turned out that she wanted to plan the next Edwardian event, and Barb started to wonder whether it would be so bad to spend lunchtimes studying in the library after all. But luckily no-one else seemed interested either—except Leith, of course.

Finally it got to Xenia that they were the only two talking. She glared round the circle. "So d'you want to do it, or don't you?"

"Xenia, it's third term," Cass said earnestly. "Mark and I, we're studying every spare minute. We just don't have time for that kind of stuff."

"Besides," mumbled Paul, pulling up clumps of grass, "I reckon it's a bit off, kids like us making out we're Toorak types, even if it's Toorak types out of history. I mean, look at the way we treated Barb, just cause she was playing the maid."

"Yeah, we all picked on her, like *Lord of the Flies*," Cass agreed, round-eyed. "I never said how sorry I was about that, Barb."

Barb shook her head, embarrassed, and Xenia said impatiently, "Well, Barb can be something else."

Mark sighed. "Typical. You just totally missed Paul's point. Well, I'll tell you why I'm not joining any more campaigns to get your picture in the paper: because I *don't want to*, so get that into your thick skull." As Xenia's black eyes swung from face to face in a desperate challenge, he went on remorselessly, "And while we're at it, how about we do some work next period, instead of listening to you rowing with Vincini again?"

"It's not my fault," blazed Xenia. "She started it."

"Well, you sure kept it going," Cass pointed out. "Honest, Xeens, you got to watch out. You know what the principal said last time."

"I couldn't give a stuff about Mr Michaels. Or Vincini. Or this whole lousy school, for that matter."

"So leave," said Paul loudly. "You're only here 'cause Mum and I talked Dad into it, anyway."

"Oh great. I can go and be a machinist like Mum," jeered Xenia. "In case you haven't noticed, I want to act."

"I've noticed," muttered Paul.

Barb couldn't stop herself from laughing. Paul grinned back, and Xenia's cheeks flushed deeper red as she gave Barb a look like sheet lightning. The siren went, but they all sat fixed to the spot until Leith gathered the cards together and stood up.

"Come on," she said matter-of-factly to Xenia. "At least you can start fighting with Vincini on time."

There was a breathless silence, till Xenia flung back her head and laughed. "You're a cool customer, Leith Dunbar," she decided and, tucking her arm through Leith's, she galloped her off to class.

Paul hung back. "Well, how'd you like having lunch with a bunch of raving loons?"

Barb hadn't been sure, but meeting his soft black eyes she said, "Beats talking to myself, so thanks for asking me. Hey, what's with Xenia these days?"

"Nothing new, she always has to push it," said Paul briefly. "See you tomorrow, then."

Barb watched him go, all long legs and flapping overcoat. He might look weird, but she reckoned he was the nicest guy she'd ever come across. With Paul as a bonus, she might even manage to put up with Xenia.

And as for Debbie Ralton, if Claudio was what she wanted, she could have him.

"Well, Xenia, I'm waiting."

"Don't know," Xenia mumbled.

"Did you read the chapter at all?"

"Nope."

"May I ask, why not?"

" 'Cause I knew you'd have a go at me anyway. So I learned my lines for the play instead."

Miss Vincini settled her gold-rimmed glasses more firmly. "Do you intend to do *any* work in this subject Xenia?" Xenia stared doggedly back. "Very well then, you can report to Mr Michaels and explain yourself to him."

"You bet I will," spat Xenia, jumping up. "I'll explain how you're trying to make me fail."

"One of us may be trying to make you fail, Xenia. But I assure you that it's not me." Behind the thick lenses Leith thought she caught a glimmer of kindness in Miss Vincini's grey eyes. She held her breath and hoped. "Now can we continue with the lesson, or would you rather see Mr Michaels?"

"Thought you said I had to." Xenia slouched out, slow and insolent, and Mark grunted, "Good riddance."

Leith agreed. Then she turned on herself in dismay. How could she pretend she loved Xenia, then start criticising her at a moment's notice? It was true, Xenia was setting herself up, and messing the whole class round in the process. But at the same time Leith's brain still rang with, "You're a cool customer, Leith Dunbar," and her body still tingled with the warm pressure of Xenia's arm.

She hid in the dunnies for a quiet moment between classes, but even there she could hear Xenia's voice.

"She not only gets me into trouble with Michaels, she makes me late for sport as well, the bastard."

Jesus, that was for real! Leith looked out cautiously, and there was Xenia, half-naked in the mirror and swearing like a trooper.

"Leith can tell you. Isn't Vincini after my guts?"

Leith gave a nothing kind of hum and scuttled past, her face on fire. That really was the pits, to criticise Xenia one minute and stare straight at her reflected breasts the next. She pushed open the swing door and pushed the thought out of her mind.

Barb wanted to rip up her maths book, but she went and made a cup of coffee instead. As she carried it carefully out the back door, there was a roar from the lounge room.

"Sue!"

She scrubbed angrily at the coffee splashed down her skirt, while Barry went on.

"I don't want to hear you giving cheek to your mother again, young lady."

You're not our dad yet, Barb told him silently, but she had to agree with her grandma: it looked as if he was planning to be, after all.

As she settled down at her desk, part of her mind was

remembering how Mum's hassles with Dad had always been over her and Sue. Maybe it was the same with Mum and Barry. Maybe that was why Barry was turning into the heavy father type.

Barb started to count the buttons on her calculator. You don't think about anything serious this close to the exams, she reminded herself. After counting the buttons five times, she started on the maths problem again. Her head was calm and lucid now, because she knew she had to pass the exams, she had to get into year 12. It was her escape route, if things got really bad.

Mark Douglas came up behind Leith in the corridor and tapped her shoulder. Leith jumped, thought, "What a giveaway," and blushed, just in case he had missed it the first time.

"Sorry. I was just wondering, did you read up any more about that woman who was murdered? 'Cause I was thinking that she's, like, the real side of the Edwardians — not all that cutesy stuff Xenia goes on about, but the dark side."

Leith talked fast to distract him from the blush still spreading across her face.

"Yeah, found out that her husband murdered his first wife and kids too, plus he was making up to another woman when they arrested him. A real psychopath. But come to think of it, I never found out much more about Emily Lydia Mather herself. She's like the body in a detective story — you need it, but the murderer's more interesting."

Mark laughed heartily. "That's great. You should get it down on paper."

Leith gradually caught on that he still wanted her to write up the story for his magazine, but he sort of, kind of, hadn't got around to asking her.

So he had been embarrassed too. It made her feel a bit better, but she still couldn't look him in the eye, so she watched the muscles on his upper arms while she told him she would see if she could get something done by Monday.

"Ripper," approved Mark.

Leith watched him go, thinking, "worse and worse". Now she was a lesbian who looked at *guys'* bodies. Someone prodded her in the ribs, and she jumped.

"Didn't want to interrupt while you were talking to Marvellous Mark. You looked pretty rapt."

Swallow gave her a sidelong look, and Leith found herself saying, "Listen, I don't know what you've been hearing, but yes, I did pash on with Mark at Gavin Petty's party, and no, I'm not seeing him or anything."

"Aha." Swallow looked pleased. "So that's why little Pammy's been down on you lately. How come you're not 'seeing him or anything', then? Thought you were in love with all that lot."

"I'm not sure how long that lot'll last," said Leith without thinking, and Swallow watched her with steady green eyes that seemed almost sorry.

Did I mean that, wondered Leith. And why talk about it to Swallow, of all people? I thought I was supposed to be trying to get away from her.

"Everything keeps changing," she complained to Barb on the way home. "You just think you've got somewhere, and it's somewhere else."

"That's life. Or else it's third term."

"Mark and Cass in the library every lunchtime. Xenia bitching on about Vincini. I'm glad you're around."

"Truly? I mean, you don't feel like I've barged in on your friends?"

"At least I can catch your eye when Xenia says something really off."

"I thought you were a big fan of Xenia's."

"I do like her," said Leith loudly. "It's just—"

"Know what you mean." Barb sighed. "Debbie keeps making cracks at me, she's even put me off going to the pub. Not that I care much. I went out with a few guys after Claudio, but never more than once. It's not that I'm scared," she explained. "I'm just not interested. Anyway, the point about Debbie is, how come I miss a creep like that?"

That's it, thought Leith sadly. When Xenia goes off into those rages, I miss her.

She thought about studying, but in the end she got out her pile of photocopies and started reading. As she pulled the few small details about Emily Lydia Mather out of the mountain of words written about her murderer, Leith started to believe more and more in what she'd said to Mark. It was wrong, how Emily had been forgotten. It was cruel.

She started to jot down words and sentences on a scrap of paper. Then she pushed the photocopies away and wrote for an hour and a half. Her hand ached, the room was dark, when she stopped, but she sat in the shadows for a while, even though she wanted to read over what she had written.

Suddenly she remembered that it was her turn to cook dinner, and a wave of unreasonable fury at her father broke over her.

Hey, no, shouted Leith, a panicky swimmer. It's not his fault. It was all tossing and tumbling together—Emily Lydia Mather dead; her mother dead; the group falling apart; Xenia so bitter and strange.

Mark was right. The dark side was the real side. The golden moment on the river, where she thought she loved everyone, was an illusion. Nothing lasts. She forgot her mother, she criticised Xenia, she was cruel; she shouldn't get close to people, not ever.

After a while Leith went unsteadily across the room to switch on the light. Cold water got her eyes back to near-normal, and her feet carried her down to the study where her father sat in a pool of light, hunched over his book.

"I forgot dinner," said Leith from the shadows. "Could you handle take-away, just this once?"

Mr Dunbar glanced up guiltily. "Actually I was wondering if it was me who'd forgotten."

"Well, it wasn't, it was me." Leith reached out with a rough protective hug, and her father smiled up vaguely, eyes still seeing the last line of print.

I used to go, "Daddy, don't die, don't you die too." I was only seven, after all. It wasn't his fault.

12
TOGETHER AND SEPARATELY

That lunchtime Cass and Mark were studying again and Xenia had dragged Leith off to hear her lines. Paul was listening to Barb's views on exams and school in general, and watching the light brown layers of her hair shift in the wind; and then she started going on about how great it was to know guys you could be friends with.

"Hang on," he mumbled. "I asked you ages ago how you'd feel if I made a pass at you."

"You never . . . When?"

"Gav's party. I obviously made a big impression." The bitter Anastasiou words were filling his mouth. Paul clenched his teeth and swallowed. "You had other things on your mind," he mumbled.

"Jesus, you're right," said Barb in wonder. "It's all coming back. I'd totally forgotten."

Now it wasn't just the bitter Anastasiou words—the black Anastasiou rage was swamping his whole body. *Forgotten! I'll get you for that, you bitch.* Paul's ears rang with raging voices and his eyes were dazzled by memories. Xenia mouthing off about Vincini; Mum screaming her heart out to the street; Dad bursting a blood vessel. *Want to be like them?*

His eyes cleared. Barb, a neat crease by each eyebrow, was still nutting it out. "I was a real mess then, probably that's why I forgot. It's not that I don't like you or anything." She looked away. "I s'pose I'm still pretty confused."

Slowly and carefully Paul unclenched his fists. "How about we try an experiment? Go to the pub or somewhere, see how it feels?"

Barb's fawn eyes widened. "I'd be in that." She didn't move, but somehow the way she was standing changed, so she seemed closer.

Don't kid yourself. That's because she feels safe now, Paul told himself. *One minute you want to murder her, next minute you're making like a baby sitter. What are ya, Anastasiou?*

"Doing anything this Friday?" he mumbled.

"Isn't there a law against having sex in public?"

Craig glared at Claudio and Debbie, plastered together in the middle of the view from their table. Claudio's hands cupped Debbie's tight jeans and their hips beat time with the drum.

Silvana was offering to change places with Barb when Paul muttered something with "dance" in it and she escaped to the far end of the dance floor. But the music kept crashing down on her heart, repeating, "Claudio. Claudio and me," and she was stranded there and her body wouldn't dance and she had to look the biggest fool of all time.

Then a warm wall was shielding her from the rest of the world. Barb leaned against Paul's black shirt and her muscles started to unknot. She could hear the steady beat of his heart more clearly than the band, and she began to wonder what he'd be like to dance with. They stepped back to face each other . . .

. . . and Claudio was there again, staring like a ghost over Debbie's shoulder. Barb stared back dumbly. Her brain didn't start working again till they were outside, leaning against the pub wall.

"Hey, you got me out, told Silv and Craig and everything. You're a pretty kind sort of person, aren't you?"

Paul gave her one of his blank looks. "With those two around, I thought we'd have a better time going downtown and watching the trendies. Okay by you?"

It was more than okay to get away from Claudio, but Barb would have liked to hang around with Silv and go over every second of the last half hour till it made sense. However she was with Paul, and he had been nice to her, so she walked close at his side and gave him some special smiles to thank him.

Being Paul, he just grinned back and got her working out which shop had the wackiest gear and which cafe had the most trendies. And, right in the middle of eating chocolate cake and playing "spot the private school kids", Barb blurted out, "So why were they following me round like that?"

Paul balanced dangerously on the back legs of his chair. "The guy's still got the hots for you. Bit hard on old Deb, though."

"No." Barb licked her finger and dabbed at cake crumbs. "No, it was Claudio who broke it off in the first place, not me. Y'know, it's sort of sad, when you think you've got something, and suddenly it's a great big nothing."

Paul's chair came forward with a crash. "I don't call it nothing, when a guy leaves a girl thinking she's a leso or frigid," he mumbled.

"That wasn't his fault, it was me thought it. Besides, after what you said, I figured I wasn't a leso anyway."

"And?"

For a moment Barb felt as if her next words were going to boom out over a public address system.

"Yeah, well, if I was wrong about one thing, I could be wrong about the other."

Paul nodded, then asked her how she felt about Claudio now, and they went over the whole thing till it made sense. As they were walking up to her front gate Barb stopped and said, "Hold on. This was supposed to be a date, and I've spent the whole night raving on about my ex-boyfriend. That's a bit off."

"Not a date, an experiment," said Paul. He followed her into the shadow of the hedge. "Want to try another one?" and he smiled.

He doesn't smile a whole lot usually, Barb realised as he bent down to kiss her. For the first time in her life she kept her eyes open. Jewel-black eyes, glitteringly close, watched her and recognised her, and she reached out, sliding her hands under the derro overcoat and gripping onto his back.

Wow. Now he's convincing me I'm not frigid.

As she thought "frigid" Barb stiffened, then swore at herself. But Paul was already moving away. "So do we carry on the experiment another time?" he asked.

"I reckon," said Barb slowly, and went from the dark front

garden into the bright lights of the house with a last kiss from Paul on her forehead.

"Who's the lucky fellow?" Barry teased.

"A friend from school."

"A boyfriend, I presume."

"Can't boys just be friends?" Barb snapped, and she marched off to the bathroom. When she came back in her dressing gown, Barry had gone and her mum was making hot chocolate.

"Did Barry put his foot in it then?" she asked.

Yeah, by being right. "It's none of his business, that's all."

"I often wish I could ask questions as directly as Barry does." Mrs O'Connell looked wistful, and Barb tucked her arm round her mum's waist.

"You don't have to, I tell you anyway." But she still wasn't ready to talk about Paul, so she told her mum about Silvana instead. "On and on and on, for the first half hour we were at the pub, about this old lounge suite her and Craig want to buy. Bor-ing."

"They're getting married, Barb. You'll be the same yourself one day."

Paul would never be into lounge suites in a million years, thought Barb. She blushed to herself. Jesus, you kiss a guy once, and next thing you're furnishing a flat with him, as if you were Trina Dunbar. He's not even my type, she reminded herself. I like him, but that's as far as it goes.

Still, whatever happened next, she knew it hadn't all ended with Claudio.

Debbie Ralton, Silvana Angostello, where are you when I need you? wailed Barb.

Paul slouched into the foyer, half a head taller than most kids, his overcoat baggy round his thin body; and Barb ducked her head and raced for her locker. Would they think I was mad to go out with him? she wondered. Would Silvana still say he looked like he hadn't eaten since he was twelve? Probably.

When she felt a tall figure at her shoulder Barb spun round, ready to show Paul he didn't own her.

"Have a good weekend?"

What are ya? thought Barb, startled. "Sure, how about you?"

"Me? Best in ages," and he winked and went.

Barb puzzled her way through maths. A weekend's dreams of kind Paul, Paul's kisses, had gone out the window. This was Monday morning, and the dreams had turned back into Paul Anastasiou with acne scars, chief dag of Central. She had been sure he would want to follow her round, like Gavin, and make everyone wonder why Barb O'Connell was going out with a weirdo. But he hadn't.

"Any questions?" asked Mr Hansen.

Barb had this crazy urge to wave her hand in the air and ask, "Sir, what were you like when you were a kid? Did you grow too fast and have pimples and that, or were you always this spunky? What should I do about Paul, sir?"

She stared hard at the textbook and kept her mouth shut.

She didn't have to worry about what to say to Paul at lunchtime because Cass was there, howling her eyes out on Xenia's shoulder.

"Hey, what's up?"

"Oh, Mark, of course." Cass lifted her face, streaked like a clown's with mascara. "He's decided he's not into heavy relationships—wish he'd thought of it sooner," and two more black tears rolled down her cheeks.

"Bastard," said Xenia fiercely.

"He went on and on about commitment, see, and I kept going, 'But we're still at school,' only then I thought, well, I really like him, so I said, 'Okay, let's give it a go.' So now he reckons I'm possessive. S'pose I just have to get uncommitted again."

"Men."

"You reckon it's genetic, Xeens?" asked Paul mildly.

"I don't mean you, ya goon," said Xenia impatiently.

Paul chuckled, and Barb nearly joined in—but not in front of Xenia's sharp eyes. So she studied her fingernails while Cass wailed, "Jesus! Why'd he have to do this three weeks before the exams?"

There's your answer, thought Barb, still looking down. You can give it a go, and maybe get done like a dinner. Or you can pass your exams, meaning you'll still be at Central next year, and see what happens then.

She met Cass's eyes. "Just try and get him out of your head," she said earnestly, but Cass didn't look as if the idea would work.

Leith was sorry for Cass, of course, but it seemed to have brought the group together again. She smiled contentedly as she half-listened to Miss Vincini's tips on exam technique. If only Swallow would ask, so she could tell her everything was fine now. But after class Swallow was busy poking fun at Pam's new plans for Mark, now Cass wasn't around. Leith laughed uneasily and sped off to join the others.

She detoured to pass a noisy group at the corner of the school building. Then she focused and saw Paul and Cass straining at each other, red-faced and shouting. Mark and Barb stood by like worried owners trying to stop a dog fight, and Con and Gavin watched with interest from the sidelines till Barb shooed them away.

"She's making a bloody mess of her life, that's why I'm mad."

"It's not her fault they were trying to expel her," protested Cass.

"They bloody weren't, it's not that easy. They were trying to get her to pull her bloody head in, but oh no! If Vincini won't kiss Xenia's feet every morning, she's walking out — to take a stinking part in a stinking soup commercial. She's pathetic!" Paul's arms dropped suddenly to his sides and he let out a long sigh. "Sorry, Cass, it's not you I should be yelling at."

Leith had followed the shouting with painful concentration, as if it was in another language. As Paul sighed again, she broke in urgently.

"Xenia's gone?"

He nodded. A sob broke out of her and she turned away. The schoolground rippled and vanished in a silver haze. Huge chunks of sobs heaved themselves up to her throat, ripping her chest as they went. She walked blindly into the dunnies and leaned against the smooth wall as she shook and retched.

Xenia's gone.

Barb listened to Cass and Paul and Mark worrying together about Xenia all lunchtime. Then as they walked through the foyer door, Cass and Mark split apart and went their separate ways again.

In the same instant Barb thought, I got it all wrong. Bad times come, whatever you do. It's crazy to turn down the good times. She looked for Paul—but what was she going to say to him?

No problems, Leith would sort her out tonight, give her the logical point of view. Barb wondered vaguely where Leith had got to at lunchtime, then she forgot about it till it was time to go home.

But after ten seconds with a stone-faced Leith she guessed that they weren't going to talk about Paul, not today.

A few blocks further on she thought some more about what had happened at lunchtime, and made another guess: Leith had stopped talking about Xenia, but she hadn't stopped thinking about Xenia.

Barb made a few tries at light chat, then she fell silent too. Usually she would have given Leith a look and gone, "So what's the hassle?" But she couldn't say it. She couldn't even look at Leith. She didn't want to know.

Barb wished wholeheartedly that the exams were over, so everything could get back to normal.

There were moments when she forgot about it and waves of time when her body was too small to hold all that pain. Leith lay on her back, looking into the dark, hearing Xenia, seeing Xenia. "You're a cool customer, Leith Dunbar." The touch of her arm— Leith turned her heard sharply, gritting her teeth against that one. Over and over Xenia moved and spoke in the closed room, till it vibrated with loss. Over and over Leith thought, I'll never see her again.

See? You let yourself care about people and they go away. Her brain shut down, and she tore at a corner of the pillow mindlessly.

A square of grey light outlined the blind. The darkness divided up into shapes and a bird chirped. Leith peered at the clock, heart pounding. *Five a.m.* She'd never seen dawn before.

The greyness oozed unstoppably into the room, the birds started to shriek at each other. Go to sleep, Leith ordered herself in a panic. The pictures of Xenia were distorted and speeded up, and a tinny little voice chattered non-stop, Nev-nev-never again.

Somewhere in the middle of the shrilling light and the dinning birds, Leith's eyes closed and she slept and dreamed fitfully.

I'll never see her again.

13
PLAYING IT COOLER

For the next few days Leith couldn't look directly at Paul; too similar, too different. Then she realised his progress reports on Xenia seemed to be aimed her way, and she remembered he had been right by her when she had first sobbed for Xenia. He's kind, thought Leith dully.

She wondered briefly whether he and Barb would get it together, then she plodded off to her next class and took her next set of notes like a robot, while Swallow poked at her and teased her with worried eyes.

"What's the matter, kid?"

"Nothing. Leave me alone."

Even when Paul was her partner at cards he didn't give her any special looks, and by the end of the week Barb had decided her first plan was the right one. See what happens next year.

"Remember how we talked about my paintings, the night of Gav's party?" Paul asked on the way back to class. "Want to come to tea sometime and have a look at them?"

"Okay."

"When?"

It was like the first time she had ever dived from the board, instead of just splashing in from the side of the pool. "I don't have a whole heap of work tonight," she said in a rush, and couldn't believe what she was hearing.

All afternoon she worked on the problem. *Barb likes to play it cool, but she practically throws herself at Paul, when she's still not sure she's interested. Why?* She studied Mr Hansen for signs that Paul would turn out like him. She watched Gavin Petty hooning round with Con in biology and wondered why you would turn down one dag, then go running after another.

Then as she rubbed shampoo through her hair under the shower at home, Barb finally got the answer. She was getting caught by her own line. She laughed and frowned and spat soapy water. The dag had played it cooler than her.

Mrs Anastasiou piled food onto her plate and smiled non-stop. Xenia gave a loud monologue on all the people who thought she was a terrific actor. When she paused for breath, older brother George fired off a series of questions about her family, and at the same time, younger sister Sofia showed her a year's drawings from school. At the end of the table Mr Anastasiou, small and stocky, ate steadily through his meal, giving her dark suspicious looks.

Paul was a hunched, blurred figure in the background. Even when he unfolded and nodded, "Come on," to Barb, George asked another question, Xenia finished her story and Mrs Anastasiou unexpectedly started to confide in her that she didn't know if the twins would ever get jobs.

Outside Barb gave him an apologetic grin. "Well, now you know the worst about me—my family," he mumbled, and strode off down the yard.

"If that's how you feel," said Barb, following, "how come you asked me over?" Paul stopped at a ladder by the garage wall and turned to face her. "Is it supposed to be some kind of test?" she asked boldly.

"I think it's some kind of confession," he said, and the smile patterned his blank face again. "Anyway, you get to see my paintings now."

Terrific, thought Barb as she scrambled up the ladder to Paul's room, the loft over the garage. Fact is, I'd rather meet someone's family than look at their paintings any day of the week. She gritted her teeth and fixed her eye on the first canvas.

Behind a vacant block covered with weeds and Coke cans, against a grey factory wall, a billboard displayed an ad for *The Edwardians*, but instead of the stars' faces her face, Leith's face, Cass and Mark stared back at her.

"Hey, it's just like us. You're good," she said, surprised. "It's about that stuff you said to Xenia, isn't it? That it was off for us to dress up as the 1890s jet set."

"Sort of. But it was interesting too, that's why I wanted to paint it," Paul muttered. "Your friend Leith, she put a lot into that day."

Barb looked closely at the neat brushstrokes that built up smooth blonde Leith. "D'you like her?"

"Sure. In a different way than I like you, though."

His arm reached out and Barb leaned into it as he explained the rest of the paintings — back streets and supermarkets, freeways and factories. His words came faster and clearer. They sat on the bed, still leaning together, hands linked, palms fitting snugly, fingers exploring. Barb laughed as Paul clowned, drew in her breath as he traced the veins of her wrist, greedily watched his face, black and gold in the half-light.

"You're mad."

Paul rolled over and stretched out along the bed. "How would you feel," he made a place beside him, "about going with a loony?" Barb laughed again as she settled down, and he kissed her lightly. "No, seriously, we're pretty different, you and me, you know."

"So?" said Barb impatiently. His mouth was a different shape when he was laughing and carrying on like this.

Paul drew the line of her cheek with one finger. "Anyhow, I can't stand that business of doing everything together, like Cass and Mark did, so I guess we could just go on being different. Yeah?"

"Yeah." *Can we kiss again? I want to see if it still turns me on.* Barb lifted her head from the pillow to help Paul slide his arm under her.

Nibbling kisses, light touches, long looks led on to long kisses, bodies folding together, hands sliding deeper. Paul kept on talking, small disjointed comments about the feel of her breasts, when he had first liked her, how bad he was at undoing buttons. The cold air pinched at them, and they crept under the bedclothes, still kissing and talking and touching. Paul groaned quietly and Barb, about to block her ears, realised she was making the same soft sounds herself.

I don't mind the noises, she realised in wonder. I don't mind him seeing me. I don't mind him hard against his jeans. I like everything.

After that, everything seemed settled. She went on seeing Paul. They agreed, right out in the open, that they wouldn't get off together till the exams were over. They held hands at school, studied together after school, kissed and caressed after studying, told their lives to each other between kisses.

Barb felt good and strong and kind. She stared Debbie down. She watched over Leith, who moved round as stiffly as if her whole body was bruised. She watched over Cass, till she cried through the first hour of the English exam, then disappeared.

Other kids cried or complained or walked round like zombies. Barb worked through the exams, as methodical as a computer, waiting for her happy ending.

She pushed past Con as he lumbered down the aisle of the exam room, head bent. She ran past Gavin, who had walked out early and was sitting on the steps, chucking stones at the rubbish bin. She clutched at Paul's arm.

"That's it for the year." Barb looked up with a teasing smile. "Now, what'll we do to celebrate?"

Paul's face was blank as the brick wall he was staring at.

"What is it?" she asked sharply.

"I couldn't tell you before." Now he looked at his feet. "Dad's decided that the only way to stop Xenia acting is to send her back to Greece for a holiday. And I'm supposed to go with her."

"Oh. Right. So when're you going?"

"Tomorrow."

As another stone clanged against the bin, Barb's mind printed out everything she had ever known about playing it cool. It was lucky she hadn't actually fallen in love with Paul. Not totally.

That night she lay awake just the same. She wanted to pull on her cotton dressing gown and pad through the heat-dazed streets to Paul's bed. She wanted to take back all her throwaway lines — "I have to warn you, I'm a lousy letter-writer . . . Sure, I'll go out with other people — you too . . . Well, see you round then."

I could have said, "I'll miss you." I could have said, "At least there's tonight."

No, I couldn't have said that, Barb corrected herself. Not in front of Gavin Petty and half of Central. Not when Paul just stood there blankly, shuffling from one foot to the other. He's the one who's supposed to say, "At least there's tonight."

Balanced uncomfortably between fury and despair, Barb thought, Oh well, he left it till after the exams, anyway.

14
"WAS IT INTERESTING, KISSING?"

Karen Swallow mooched out the backyard where her brothers were taking a motorbike apart. She watched them for a while, then decided to mow the lawn. The racket of the motor mower drowned out her thoughts for a while, but as soon as she stopped, the boredom pressed back in. Swallow leaned against a tree and tried to work out some way to get out of the city, and someone to escape with.

Or someone to do anything with. Jeff and Wayne and Pete were fine if you wanted to fix a bike. Trina was fine if you wanted to talk about getting married. Pam was fine if you wanted to whinge. The parents were fine if you wanted to watch TV and grunt about your hard day at work. If you just wanted some reasonable conversation, that left Leith.

Swallow kicked the tree deliberately and waited for the dull ache to spread across her toes. Bloody Leith, going off with the Anastasiou crowd, that pack of nerds. She flexed her toes thoughtfully. On every side of her, rows of houses spread out, full of people fixing bikes and watching TV and getting married and whingeing. Standing in the backyard in her T-shirt and blue jeans, Swallow felt very small and very noticeable at the same time.

I'm not that special, she thought in a panic. There ought to be a few more like me around.

As if Leith was actually there, Swallow twitched at the irritating way her blonde hair wisped out from her pony tail, the irritating way she assumed everyone had read all the books in her dad's bookcases. Let her ring me for a change, she decided. But she went inside to the phone all the same.

"Oh, it's you," said Leith gloomily.

"What's up?"

"Nothing."

"What's down, then?"

"Me, I s'pose."

"Hmm?" Swallow probed, but Leith said nothing. "Well, why don't you come round and watch the new mini-series on TV? It sounds so depressing, it might cheer you up."

"Thanks, but —"

"Just 'Thanks' will do," said Swallow grandly. "Me and me dad can pick you up at five-thirty, but the snag is, the parents are going to a union dinner—actually, you're their idea of a cheap baby sitter."

"Oh yeah? So you're their idea of a cheap baby?"

Swallow gave her deep chuckle. "Dead right, kid. Anyhow, if you'll let me finish, they won't be home till eleven-thirty, which means . . ."

"Six hours with their cheap baby for me. Oh well, we'll have the teev."

"Not only beautiful, but she can add as well," marvelled Swallow. "I see you later, dollink."

Leith went up to her room and cried because Swallow wasn't Xenia. She sponged the tears away with weary patience and sat on the bed working her hanky like a soggy concertina. It wasn't fair. She had got it all clear in her mind that she would never see Xenia again. Then there she had been, racing off to her last exam, and zap—she was face-to-face with Xenia.

"I want to talk to you, Leith Dunbar," she'd said. "I'll ring you." But she hadn't. And then Swallow had told her that Xenia and Paul were in Greece. Swallow, not Barb, which was a bit odd, but Barb was working in Barry's office over the holidays, so she probably didn't have much spare time. Which was fine by Leith. If she couldn't see Xenia, she didn't want to see anyone.

Mind you, it could get pretty boring, doing nothing but cry, eat double-decker sandwiches and read through the next load of library books. But even so, a night of Swallow jokes and insults was the last thing she needed.

To start with, she got the entire Swallow family. Jeff and Wayne and Pete marching to and fro, shouting orders and asking where everything was. Mrs Swallow popping in and out, in various stages of getting dressed, to shout back, "Do it yourself," and, "In the usual place." Then she or Swallow impatiently pushing in to do it faster.

Leith shielded herself behind Mr Swallow, who was waiting stiffly at the table in his new suit. But then he started asking her about her exam results—"You did pretty well, then. Hope some of it rubs off on Karen"—and Mrs Swallow called her in to pick a necklace for her—"You've got a bit of dress sense, Leith, you should take Karen shopping some day, get her out of those dreadful jeans."

How do they manage to keep track of everything that's going on, wondered Leith, sifting through the jewel box. All the noise and shouting—if my father yelled at me like that, I'd jump out of my skin, but you can tell they're not really mad or anything.

She followed Mrs Swallow back to the kitchen and, as she and Mr Swallow looked at each other with satisfaction, Leith's eyes suddenly prickled with tears again. Not here, you can't cry here, she told herself savagely. Specially when there's nothing to cry about.

Then everyone left at once. Leith, dazed by the sudden silence, sat and watched as Swallow lounged round the kitchen getting their tea together. They started to chat about who had passed and who had failed the exams, the subjects they would like to take next year, books they had been reading and films they had seen on TV. Leith remembered how much she liked Swallow's wisecracks, when they weren't aimed at her.

As they settled down in front of the TV with plates of chicken and salad, Swallow remarked, "Just like old times, hey? You're all right when you're not running round after Xenia and her lot."

Leith plunged straight into paranoia. Was that why Xenia hadn't got in touch, because she thought Leith was running round after her? By the first commercial, she had managed to remind herself that she hadn't asked Xenia to ring, Xenia had offered. And she could hardly phone from Greece.

No, it was just Swallow taking a dig at her, as usual. How come someone with such kind, friendly parents spent their whole life going for the jugular? An exaggeration, Leith admitted. Swallow could be friendly too; she had even been kind to her lately, in her own way.

But all of this was distracting her from missing Xenia. Leith started to make up for lost time, chanting, *Xenia, Xenia Anastasiou* like a charm in the spaces between the actors' lines.

After the show Swallow towed her off to her bedroom to see her new two-volume dictionary. "Sit down," she ordered, as Leith hovered by the bed, feeling large. "And don't perch."

Leith hitched herself forward a few centimetres and listened as Swallow read out all the definitions that had anything to do with sex. "Which reminds me," she grinned, "heard any juicy gossip since term ended?"

Leith scanned weeks bare of interest in anyone bar Xenia. "Oh yeah, Jan Leslie came marching up to me in the newsagent's last week and said to tell Xenia she was going out with some guy. Don't know what all that was about."

Swallow sat up and scowled. "Ah, she's letting herself be pushed around, but she'll get over it."

"What d'you mean, pushed around?" Too late, it sank in that Swallow'd got mad last time they talked about Jan. Wrong bit of gossip.

Swallow was eyeing her levelly. "You should know. You were helping to push."

Leith felt five steps behind. She remembered sitting in Barb's garden, joking with Xenia. "Lesbie friends" . . . But that wasn't supposed to have any effect on *Jan*.

"I was lovers with Jan for a while, round the time we were going bushwalking," said Swallow conversationally.

A hidden trapdoor opened and dropped Leith into another world where the light was brighter, the walls closed in, and Swallow was surrounded by a crackling field of static electricity.

"Well?" came her voice insistently, while Leith was still blinking. "Aren't you going to say something?"

Why not, thought Leith. It's another world. "I can't exactly disapprove, if that's what you mean, 'cause I'm in love with Xenia." Her brain started to speed. "You should've told me, and I wouldn't have said all that about Jan."

"So what, if you were thinking it? Besides, it's not the easiest thing in the world to tell someone."

Leith was getting used to the new light. She found and focused on Swallow's eyes. "What d'you think about me and Xenia, then?" she asked urgently.

"If you're into neurotic, attention-seeking posers, you've picked the right girl."

"Ah, she isn't. Well, maybe, but . . ."

"Go on, you can tell Auntie Swallow."

As Leith talked the room opened out again and Swallow sat cross-legged at its centre, listening steadily and nodding. Leith felt as light as air. She waited hopefully for some wise or helpful words, but Swallow just said, "So you never got off with her?"

"I wasn't trying to. I just wanted to be around." Leith thought about it. "Does that make me weird, even for a lesbian?"

"No, I know what you mean," said Swallow reluctantly.

"Are you still in love with Jan?" The blood rang in Leith's ears. She wanted to hear Swallow's story, she wanted to tell her own story again, she wanted to talk and talk and never stop.

"No," said Swallow. "I wasn't ever in love with Jan."

"But you said you knew what I meant."

"Can I kiss you?" Swallow asked. She leaned forward gravely and pressed warm dry lips against Leith's. When she moved back she was still small, solid Swallow. "Now you kiss me."

Leith lurched forward on the spring mattress and dabbed a kiss near Swallow's mouth. She couldn't feel anything except the pounding that shook her whole body.

"You're shivering."

Thanks for telling me.

Leith clenched herself, then squinted through half-closed eyes and lined up her mouth and Swallow's, because she didn't know what she would say to her if they stopped. A flicker of memory brought back the dreamy feeling from when she had kissed with Mark, and her lips parted. Then Swallow twisted round beside her and they tumbled together in a sprawl of arms and legs. Leith gulped at the air and kissed again. And kissed again.

You could kiss quickly or slowly. Your tongues were pointed one minute, round and soft the next. They touched glossy teeth or the ridged roof of the mouth or the silky cushions of the cheeks. Your lips could kiss small and sharp, or press so closely that they drew both bodies with them. It was hide-and-seek in a huge warm space; play, or very serious. But it's me and Swallow, Leith realised, and her eyes flew open.

Swallow stared back, edged away. "D'you want to talk about it?" Her hair was ruffled, her face soft, and Leith was staring in wonder at the shape of her mouth when she snapped, "I just thought you might be freaked, okay?"

"It'd take more than you to freak me, kid," Leith answered automatically, and Swallow jumped off the bed.

"Damn, that's the parents' car." She glanced back at Leith. "Your hair looks like a haystack."

"Well, your bed looks like a cyclone hit it."

Swallow tugged at the corners of the bedspread, Leith smoothed a layer of hair across the knots, and they were out in the lounge room when the front door clicked. At the last minute they leaned together and kissed swiftly; and Mr and Mrs Swallow came in seconds later.

Leith walked the house for a while, then she started to write down everything that had happened the night before. When she came to the part where they kissed, something scrabbled inside her, its arms pushing on her breasts, its feet kicking at her groin.

She tore up the foolscap pages and threw them away. Ring, Swallow, she commanded. The phone crouched beside her, waiting. *Ring Swallow? But I don't know what to say.*

She was dialling, Swallow was answering, and in between the silences they arranged to meet in the park; houses seemed like a danger zone.

Little kids swarmed the slides and monkey bars, buzzed through the air on swings, fell over and howled thinly, while Swallow leaned against a tree and watched Leith's efforts to get a conversation going.

I don't know what I'm doing here, thought Leith, and then

her voice was wobbling out. "Are you mad with me?"

One eyebrow flickered. "I thought we were making polite chat."

"Well, we're not," Leith choked.

"Do go on."

"What did you think about last night?" Leith was hit by another attack of the shakes. *Did it really happen, Swallow? Tell me it's all right, you've got to tell me it's all right.*

Swallow smiled tightly to herself. "The show was interesting, we had some interesting chats."

"Was it interesting, kissing?"

"Yes, as a matter of fact." Swallow's chin jutted. "Did you find it interesting?"

"I liked it," said Leith. Her mouth trembled.

After a moment Swallow's hand nudged hers in the grass. Leith stilled in surprise. I didn't come here to decide. I've decided, she admitted to herself, eyes fixed on the kids' zig-zag. Their fingers closed and rubbed together, as regular and steady as if they were working a fire stick between them.

Leith wanted to kiss Swallow again, but she could have sat there forever, heavy with wanting; except that a kid on a bike swerved to miss them and their hands jumped and they turned to look at each other.

"Well, then," said Swallow gruffly.

"Why were you all distant in the park?"

"Listen, kid, I'd kissed you, hadn't I? You could've spread it all round Central that I was a leso—I wasn't about to set myself up even further by putting heavies on you."

"But I'm a lesbian too." Leith stroked Swallow's bare shoulders, smoother and whiter than she'd ever have guessed, and Swallow twisted her head round to grin at her.

"So how was I to know?"

"D'you know now?" Leith smiled proudly, but her smile died as soft shoulders shrugged against her breast.

"Maybe."

"Maybe?" repeated Leith, wounded.

"Listen, people have been known to lead lesbians on for kicks, like that bitch Katie Watson did to Jan, for example."

Leith frowned at the giant teddy bear watching her from Swallow's chest of drawers. She had never understood the girl/boy rules, as Barb and Mark had both pointed out. So what if there were rules for being lesbian that she couldn't understand either?

"Mind you, after the last two hours I'd have to say you weren't just leading me on," Swallow observed, and Leith sighed with relief. Then she could feel Swallow shaking with silent giggles.

"What's the matter now?"

"Last night," Swallow got out at last, "last night when you were talking to Mum, I went past and I heard her say" . . . She broke down again for a while, and Leith prodded her impatiently. "I heard her say, 'If only you could get Karen out of those dreadful jeans.'"

Leith stared for a moment, then blushed, then started to giggle too. "Karen Swallow, you've got a filthy mind."

"But you love it," Swallow pointed out.

All the time they were getting dressed they joked together more and more wildly. Leith felt as if all the rules in the world had been repealed. Like the last day of classes, but with the sudden pangs of fear that said exams were still to come.

Then, as she untangled her hair with Swallow's brush for the second time in two days, Swallow said casually behind her, "See you tomorrow then?" and the fear slid straight into joy.

Halfway through getting changed Leith went and found the gilt-handled mirror her aunt had given her years ago. She propped it against a heap of bedclothes, took a deep breath and spread her legs. The mirror showed her a divided mound furred with light brown curls. Leith opened the mound carefully and sharp pleats of wrinkled rose-pink flesh slid forward. It looked weird. Leith frowned and made herself unfold the pleats.

Up lifted a flame-shaped point. Leith stroked it and found a pearly centre. For a moment she was stretched on Swallow's bed, eyes gaping, body leaping. That's where she touches, so small, how does she know? Leith rolled the pearl under her finger. *How will I find hers? Is everyone the same?*

A door slammed. Leith shoved the mirror under her pillow, hurled herself into her shorts and clattered downstairs. Her father was at the kitchen table, unfolding the paper.

"Too hot in my office—I came home to work," he explained.

"Fine, I'm going to a film with Barb anyway." Leith cut a slice of bread while Mr Dunbar nodded approvingly at a Tandberg cartoon. "Did you decide about going away?" she asked through a mouthful.

"Was I deciding something?"

"Well, you didn't seem too keen on the idea."

"I did point out that it's a long way, especially for two girls on their own, and that you're not an experienced camper. But it's your decision, Leith."

"I'd really like to . . ."

"That's settled then," and he went on with the paper.

Stranded behind her father's back, Leith got a sudden flash of throwing her arms round him and going, "I want to stay with you, Daddy." Where did that come from? She shook her head and went to ring Swallow.

They talked for half an hour, first making lists of camping gear, then a few careful jokes about not having seen each other for a whole day. Two weeks had passed since their first kiss, two weeks of holiday afternoons with the sun shining through bedroom windows. They'd worked out lots of new ways of touching in that time, but they hadn't exactly found the new words to go with them yet.

Leith had to find words for Barb too. She had planned heaps of opening lines, but in the end she didn't get to use any of them because they met up with some friends of Barb's from Central and went to a pancake place with them afterwards. And you couldn't tell your best friend you were a lesbian when you were halfway home on the tram.

As they walked down the block to Leith's house Barb said abruptly, "You know how I was going with Paul at the end of third term?"

"I had lunch with you every day, I could hardly miss it," Leith pointed out.

"Well, he wrote to me from Greece and I couldn't think what

to say, so, well, I haven't answered."

"Oh, right," said Leith, puzzled. Then she caught on: I say "mm", she talks about Paul.

As Barb started to recite Paul's letter word for word she wanted to say, "Barb, I can't stop thinking about Swallow either—does everyone feel like that? We keep starting to talk and ending up in a clinch—is it like that for you too?

"Another thing—how do you know if you're in love with someone? With Swallow, it's not the same as with Mark—I mean, I really like her—but it's not the same as Xenia either—I sure as hell don't think Swallow's perfect.

"And what does it mean, being a lesbian? Was I a lesbian already when I was in love with Xenia, or not till I got off with Swallow? And if sex makes the difference, why was I so secret about loving Xenia, when I couldn't give a stuff about what people think about me actually getting off with Swallow?"

Except, of course, I'm only saying this in my head, Leith reminded herself. I still haven't told my best friend Barb that I'm on with Swallow. Because I'm scared, or because she doesn't like Swallow, or because we're only ten steps from my front door?

Barb flicked a quick glance at the house too, and started to fish around in her bag. As Leith opened the door, she pushed a white envelope into her hand.

"Look at it later."

Leith read the note first.

> *Been meaning to give you this for ages— it was just lying round in Paul's room and I figured you might as well have it. — Barb.*

She edged the glossy photo out of the envelope and Xenia smiled up at her.

Instantly it was like losing her all over again. *Oh, Xenia.— Oh, Swallow.* The two sighs battled inside her, then were blown away by a third. *Oh, Barb. Thank you.*

But somehow it made it even harder for her to say, "It's not Xenia any more. It's Swallow."

15
NEXT STEP?

"Have you done lots of hitching?"

"Why?"

Leith grinned. Other things may have changed, but Swallow stayed naturally suspicious. "Just wondered, that's why."

"Jan and I hitched a bit. And I hitched by myself once, with these guys who thought I was a boy the whole way."

"That's great!"

"No, it wasn't."

Leith stared up at the stars, counting her mistakes. Scared of hitching, ignorant about putting up tents and making fires, bad at following orders, just said the wrong thing again. But the fact was, she still wanted to be here. So she blinked at the sky and decided to get her act together.

"What d'you mean, Swallow?"

"Well, having small tits and liking my hair short doesn't mean I'm a bloke, does it? How would you like it if people kept chasing you out of loos? 'This is the *Ladies*, sonny.'"

"Fair enough. But at least then they wouldn't be whistling and making comments about your big tits. I like your small tits," said Leith, at the same time as Swallow said, "I like your big tits."

They laughed and moved closer together. "We'd be more comfortable in the tent," Swallow pointed out after a while, but once they had settled down on the double sleeping bag, she started complaining that Leith's hands had got cold.

"S'pose I'll have to rub them for you."

"All of me's cold," whinged Leith.

"You want me to rub all of you?"

"Great idea."

As Swallow knelt and busily warmed Leith's back her breasts tilted softly forward and Leith reached up through the darkness to cup and cuddle them. So Swallow tumbled onto her and they rolled this way and that, hands stroking, legs gripping tightly. They curled together and kissed, and then Swallow stretched full length, down Leith's body, rounding handfuls of her breasts and lifting her nipples with her tongue. Leith grabbed her waist and pulled her even closer as her breasts began to tower and the dark country night spun around her.

"Karen. Karen. Karen."

As she cried out, a wind tugged at the canvas, and as soon as she could move, Leith had to find the torch and check that the tent was still safe. She ran the circle of light over Swallow's bare shoulders and Swallow smiled up at her.

It's about time I touched her the way she touches me.

As Leith kissed along the streamlined muscles of Swallow's breasts, her hand travelled confidently downwards. At the last minute she panicked. *What if I hurt her?* But her fingers became patient, pressed this way and that: and then she was living in the pad of one fingertip, slipping and sliding till she found the point where Swallow sighed and settled herself more firmly. Then Leith remembered the rest of her body and fitted herself closely to Swallow, moving as she moved, all of it faster and faster, until Swallow made a small surprised noise and arched against her and kicked out.

And the tent started to fall down.

"Grab the pole, quick."

The canvas sagged and rocked. Swallow clung to one pole, Leith to the other. They struggled wildly for balance; and then they were in a tent again. As Leith collapsed, naked and puffing, Swallow's voice said drily, "Did the earth move for you too, kid?"

When they could stop laughing they decided they were starving and scrambled over to raid the food bag.

"I'm wide awake," said Leith happily, and kissed Swallow to prove it.

Swallow leaned back, smiling. Without her clothes she always looked quite different; or maybe it was the watchful look in her eyes that had gone. Leith wriggled down and fitted herself into the curve of Swallow's shoulder. Another difference. In bed she could be smaller than Swallow when she wanted.

"Okay, what'll we talk about?" she demanded.

"Moments like these, you're meant to tell the story of your life, but we know most of that stuff already." Swallow paused. "One thing I never asked you. D'you miss your mum much?"

"Wish I did, in a way. I've been talking to my father about her lately, seeing I don't remember much myself. He said she was the kind of person who had to try everything—like flying lessons!—but she was really nervous too, and that was why she was so brave. If you see what I mean."

"Sounds nice."

"Yeah," said Leith sadly. "So what about your folks? What do you think of them?"

"Get on well with m'dad. Mum—I dunno. She has these three sons, see, then finally she gets a daughter and thinks, great, I can dress her up and talk girl-talk with her and that—and gradually she realises that what she's got is me. You have to feel sorry for her."

"No, I don't," said Leith indignantly, with a series of quick kisses against Swallow's throat. "She ought to count herself lucky. Anyway, how come she has ideas like that when she's got a job herself?"

Swallow laughed. "Dad reckons she's got two jobs—work and the union. She reckons, add us and make it three. Look, she wouldn't *make* me wear dresses. It's just that she likes all that stuff herself, so she would've liked me to like it too."

"Hmm. Still seems a bit contradictory."

"So? What about your old man explaining to me that time about how philosophy wasn't some airy-fairy thing, it was about how people really lived their lives? He keeps well away from real people all the same. A bit contradictory, hey?"

"That's not true!" Leith found herself stuck for proof. "Um. He likes it when my friends come round. And there aren't whole lots of relatives on his side of the family." She thought again. "I s'pose you're right. He is a bit of a hermit."

"Wowee! Leith admits she's wrong."

"Don't I do that often?"

"No way."

"Tell me about it."

More answers and more questions, in between more kisses and touches. Then a bird sputtered and Leith looked up to see the canvas walls glowing grey.

Dawn! All at once her pulse was racing. She was trapped in the night she had spent mourning for Xenia. She buried her head in Swallow's side, and Swallow looked up and yelped, "Jesus, Leith Dunbar, we've just told the story of our lives after all."

Leith drew in a long breath. "Well, it's different now."

As they were settling comfortably round each other, Swallow suddenly twisted back to look at her. "One last thing. Why'd you call me Karen before?"

"Dunno. Swallow just didn't sound right for, y'know, then."

"Well, it's what you call me the rest of the time. I don't like you changing it."

"Fair enough. G'night, Swallow."

"Don't you mean, good morning?"

They crawled out of the tent at twelve, stupid with the heat, and stumbled around finding wood for a fire. Leith gave up in the end and sat blearily watching Swallow cook.

"The billy's boiling—you could at least make the tea. You're not an Edwardian lady with a maid now, y'know."

Leith reached out and burned her fingers on the wire handle. "Jesus, you harp on about that Edwardian stuff," she snapped.

"Well, it really pissed me off. I mean, you went to so much trouble, reading all those books, making all the gear, and you weren't even putting on a play or something at the end of it. Pointless." Swallow sat back on her heels, shaking her head as she dished up breakfast.

"Hang about." The machinery of Leith's brain started up slowly. "Paul did a painting, and Mark might write a poem, for all I know. Besides, the whole thing was what Xenia said, living theatre. Like, it showed you how people could live with style, and beautiful things, and make something out of their ordinary lives."

Swallow snorted. "Listen, kid, anyone can live with style and beautiful things on a private income, though I suppose that idea's a bit basic for you clever lot. Anyway, what d'you mean, *Mark* might write about it? How about you?"

"Me?" Leith stalled. "Why do you want me to write about it, when you think it's so terrible?"

"That's not the point," said Swallow impatiently, scrubbing at her plate with a crust of bread. "It means something to you, any fool could see that."

Before she could look up, Leith said quickly, "Well, I did write something."

She started to explain to Swallow how she had tried to find out about Emily Lydia Mather and found out about her murderer instead, and how she had tried to turn the spotlight back onto Emily Lydia again.

"Hey, I've got an idea," Swallow interrupted eagerly. "This friend of my mum's helps put out this sort of women's lib magazine—it's quite good. Maybe you could send your story to them."

"But I wrote it for Mark's magazine."

"So send it to both."

Leith frowned. "I don't think that's the sort of thing you do."

"The sort of thing you do," mimicked Swallow. She jumped up and went to hurl her plate back in the tent. "You make me spew sometimes, you're so middle class. 'Oh, I couldn't do that, it's not proper manners.'"

Leith sat still as stone. "What d'you mean, middle class?"

"Your dad works at the uni, and you need to ask what bloody class you are?"

"My father is not middle class," Leith fired. "His father was just as much of a blue collar worker as your folks."

Swallow sighed. "You just don't get the point, do you? I sometimes wonder why you aren't off at a posh school with all the other professors' daughters."

"My father doesn't believe in private schools, and neither do I. But I s'pose I'm missing the point again." Leith got up shakily. "I think I'll go for a walk now."

She blundered off to the road, looked round desperately and found a track leading up the hill.

I'm not middle class, she insisted. I don't fit in with my Hartley cousins, going off to Noumea with the school to practise their French. I don't want me to be on one side and Swallow on the other. Why does she have to pick on me all the time?

The track climbed through scrub, then pushed her out into an eye-level view of mountain tops, woolly with blue-green eucalypts, elbowing each other into the distance. Above her a green curve of hill planted with a thousand gum trees, below her a blackberry gully threaded by a scurrying brown creek, ahead a flat blue sky.

All right, Leith thought more calmly, Swallow picked on me, but I snapped back. It all seems to prove that I don't really love her, not the way I loved Xenia. She pushed through a fall of leaves and whimpered as they whipped her face.

I still couldn't bear never to sleep with her again.

She trudged on up the track, and the gum trees folded her into their crevices of moist shade. Ferns sprouted up and a thin waterfall trickled between birdcalls. Leith decided that she was a hermit like her father, not used to other people. Loving Xenia from a distance might have hurt, but at least it was safe. Swallow, on the other hand, was right up close.

Face it, you made a mistake, Leith told herself reasonably. She'll agree, she's obviously getting sick of me too, picking fights like that. We'll break it off in a friendly, sensible way, and I can go back to where I was before.

She was stumbling down the hillside, skidding on pebbles, stubbing her toe against tree roots, sending out distress calls: wait for me, Swallow, wait. Sweaty and breathless, Leith thumped back into the view of mountains, and an invisible chorus of kookaburras burst into a roar of laughter.

She glared, then grinned reluctantly. "Oh, all right, it looks like I do like her."

So what about the class stuff? she wondered, the beat of her feet getting slower and more regular. What about the Edwardians? Stupid to fight about them, really; they were just a kind of dream.

Just something to offer Xenia? No, that day on the river had meant something, something she was scared she might lose if she went on talking to Swallow.

Tough luck—that's what Swallow would say.

"Tough luck," said Leith out loud.

She ran the last few metres to the road, then stood still, feeling shy. Act casual, she told herself. The camp site was empty, but she found Swallow splashing about in the river.

"Come on in, it's great."

"No, it isn't, it's freezing," said Leith, waiting till her feet were used to the water before she took the next step.

"Just dive, go under all at once. You'll feel much better."

Leith shook her head and carefully took a second step. Four more slow steps had her up to her waist and Swallow charging over to dunk her by force.

"Lay off. This is my way of doing it, thanks very much."

"Oh well, we couldn't try anything different, could we?" and Swallow swam off sulkily again.

Leith watched the curls and coils of the current and waded forward till the water covered her breasts. When Swallow paddled back she said quickly, "Listen, this class stuff, we'll talk about it again later?" A nod. "Just tell me, is it really that important?"

Swallow shrugged. "Sometimes. So what?" Her green eyes caught the sun. "Look, you're making these incredible patterns, all white under the water. Beautiful."

"Me?"

"Who else?" She flicked a spray of water at Leith. "I can't stand it, get under," she snapped.

She does that all the time when it's about feelings, Leith realised. Picks a fight or makes a joke or rushes off. It's a big cover up, and I thought it was natural cool.

To hid her pleased grin she took a deep breath and sank. Swallow caught her as she surfaced and they swayed together in a slippery hug.

"D'you reckon we'll go on being together?" Swallow's voice deep against Leith's breastbone.

Next step: if it's a big cover up, I could hurt her.

No, not me, Leith argued back quickly. I'm the one who gets hurt, not the one who hurts other people.

She looked down. Swallow's hair was sleek and wet, her face hidden.

Next step?

16
SO EASY, THEN

"You're probably sitting there thinking, 'Here comes another year of the same old grind.'"

Kids nodded and grinned, waiting for the punchline.

"Well, you're wrong," Mr Hansen told them sternly. "HSC's like no other year. For starters, this year you're going to *work*."

Barb joined in the general groan, but already she was frantically figuring out how on earth she was going to fit more work in. For example, it was a good thing she wouldn't be going out with Paul Anastasiou.

Paul, who was somewhere in Central at this very minute, not looking for her, because he would assume she wasn't interested. If only she had answered that letter, Barb sighed. It would have been so easy, then.

"And if any of you think I've turned into a slave driver overnight," Mr Hansen was saying, "let me just remind you that it's your futures we're talking about."

Besides, Barb told herself, I'm still mad at him for the way he told me about Greece. The least he could have done was write one more letter.

Leith had sped back to Central, feet hardly touching the pavement. She skimmed the crowd in the foyer and found Swallow's black-cat's-fur head straight away. Leith homed in—a week apart was a long time—and blindfolded Swallow with her hands.

"Guess who?"

Swallow was out of reach in a second. "Who else'd be that stupid?" she hissed.

Leith stared back, slowly turned away. Swallow hurried to catch up with her.

"Leith, calm down, I missed you too, I didn't want to go

on any bloody family holiday. But we can't have the big reunion scene in the middle of Central. We'd be crucified."

Leith gave her a quick scornful look.

"It's the truth, Leith. Remember Jan and Katie."

"But we're on together. That's different."

Swallow edged her into a quiet corner. "Leith—" she stood there, her pale face creased and shadowed. Finally she said, "Look, play it my way till we can talk about it, okay."

Leith hunched her shoulders and frowned back. "Sure. Sure."

While Miss Vincini raved on about how hard HSC was going to be, Leith slumped at her desk and tried to make her mind a blank. Then books started to fan open all round her, and she tugged at Kylie Carter's sleeve to ask for the page number.

"Keep your hands off me, Leith Dunbar."

Leith shook her head. Swallow was getting her paranoid now, she was imagining this strange knowing look in Kylie's eyes. She found her place by peering over the shoulder of the kid in front, and went back to her argument with Swallow.

As she filed out of class she felt strange looks in the air again. And you're growing hairs on your palms too, she scoffed, but she turned in relief as Jackie Reilly came up to her.

"What's the matter with you then?" asked Jackie roughly.

"Huh?"

"I said, what's the matter with you? Pretty simple question."

"I'm fine. Why?"

" 'Cause I reckon anyone who goes with girls has to be sick, that's why."

Leith, feeling sick, watched helplessly as Jackie strode away. Kylie waited for her, grinning congratulations, and in the background Pam Wagner's round eyes met hers with secret glee.

"Trust you to pick Mark Douglas to muck around with," snarled Swallow.

Pam, Kylie and Jackie had followed them right across the park, making loud comments and kissing noises. Then they had discussed the dangers of sitting too close to lesos and sauntered off, nudging each other and snickering.

"What's Mark got to do with it?"

"You have to ask? Why else has little Pammy got it in for you?"

"Well, you're not exactly her favourite person either."

Swallow looked grimly in her direction, face set. Leith started to apologise, but then she checked and, sure enough, Swallow had her eye on Pam and the others. They'd joined up with some other kids, and all of them were looking their way.

"Someone must've seen us together in the holidays."

Swallow jumped to her feet. For a moment the other group's eyes swivelled away, but whispers and bursts of smothered laughter followed them as they headed off across the park.

"We're running away."

"Rather sit there and take it, kid?"

"There's got to be something we can do. Like, um, talking to them."

"Saying precisely what? 'Boo hoo, don't be nasty to us.'"

"Something." I'll ask my father, thought Leith; but then that didn't seem such a good idea.

It was like one of those dreams where you try to run and your legs won't move. Barb had taken ages to get from class to her locker, from her locker to the top of the stairs. As she leaned there, this amazing guy strolled across the foyer. He was tall, good-looking and Paul Anastasiou.

Barb got herself together and started to move, slow and graceful, down the stairs, all the time thinking: what's he done to himself? Put on a bit of weight, his skin's cleared, he's left that daggy coat at home. He looks stunning.

"Oh, Paul, I couldn't find you anywhere. I wanted to ask you about Greece. You look like you had a grouse time."

Katie lingered admiringly over the compliment and Barb, halfway down the stairs, decided she had forgotten something from her locker after all. As she turned away, she figured out that she hadn't just been a fool, she'd been a FOOL. Now that Paul had

the Katie Watson Seal of Approval—
"Barb! Barb O'Connell!"

"But why?" Leith demanded. "Why, why, why?"

"Oh, hi, Trina," said Swallow clearly.

Trina settled down beside them, laying out her lunch and books carefully, while Leith beamed "Get lost" messages at her red-gold head. Trina looked up brightly.

"Well, I gather Pam's hanging round with Jackie and Kylie this year. No great loss."

Swallow's eyebrows winged up. "If you say so."

"Now, time for business. I know you two were away for my engagement party, but Jeff's twenty-first's coming up soon and I wondered, if I said you didn't have to wear a dress," she twinkled at Swallow, "or have one of my brothers as a partner," she twinkled at Leith, "whether you two would come along together?"

"Does that mean we dance together?" asked Swallow, poker-faced.

Leith flashed a warning look, but Trina just chuckled gently. "Oh, I don't think Jeff's mum could cope with that, Swallow. But please come, I really want my friends there."

"Okay," said Leith, at the same time as Swallow muttered, "Maybe."

Trina rewarded them with a smile like polished apples and opened her physics book. Leith and Swallow swapped bemused looks over her head.

"How was Greece?" Barb kicked herself for using Katie's line.

"Fine," mumbled Paul. "Long way away, but."

"Maybe that's why I couldn't write," said Barb unguardedly, and kicked herself again.

"I kept thinking, maybe your letter got lost in the post."

"No . . ."

"But I s'pose if I'd really thought that, I'd have written again."

Barb looked up at last. "I kept thinking, maybe your second letter got lost in the post."

Leith was hoping she would get a chance to talk to Swallow on the way back to class, but for some reason Trina walked her right to her locker. She shouldered past Pam and Jackie, then fixed them with a bright blue stare until they trailed away silently.

"Take no notice of them."

"But I can't—"

"Yes, you can," said Trina, kind but firm.

They were getting nowhere fast when the siren went.

"Well, I'll see you round," said Barb hopelessly. With Katie Watson, maybe.

Paul gave her his broad, beautiful smile and, while Barb was wondering why they wrote *Cinderella* about a girl, he was saying, "Yeah. How about tonight after school, for example?"

Barb stood there, dumbstruck. He looked down at his feet and mumbled, "Unless you're seeing someone else, I mean."

Suddenly her voice came back with an explosive, "No." She couldn't stop smiling. "No, that's fine."

Neither Pam, Jackie nor Kylie were in Leith's last class, so she could only guess what they might do next. She gathered up her books with shaking hands, and turned the corner to her locker breathless with fright.

No-one there. Which didn't prove they weren't waiting for her somewhere else. Leith held tight to the locker door with drowning strength, but there was no choice. She couldn't stay here till the cleaners swept her out. She had to find Swallow; and Barb to say she wasn't walking home with her.

All the same, her heart kicked her throat every time someone overtook her in the corridor, and she sidled through the plate glass doors like a TV hero under fire.

No ambush here either. Bouncy with relief, Leith headed for the corner, then came to a tactful halt as she saw Barb talking earnestly to Paul. Barb's hand lifted tentatively, and Leith dug her nails into her palm.

Go on, Paul, go on, she barracked silently.

Then as he opened his arms her eyes suddenly smarted with

anger and she turned away before he pulled Barb, smiling, towards him.

I felt like that too, this morning, thought Leith. It seemed like a long time ago.

17
READY OR NOT

Barb checked to make sure she had packed all her things for school, then she dug out the plastic strip from her underwear drawer. She popped the last yellow pill from the foil and swallowed it, thinking, "Here goes, ready or not."

She raced over to the park at lunchtime, but Mark was there already, talking to Paul.

"So what was this big shock?"

Mark signalled not wanting to say in front of Barb, but Paul kept waiting patiently for an answer.

"Ah, nothing much. Just that I was ribbing Nick about something he said in class, and all of a sudden he goes, 'So your old girlfriend's a leso?' Turns out he meant Leith Dunbar, though I dunno why anyone would think she was my girlfriend."

"Unless they'd seen you make a heavy pass at her," Barb said coldly.

"Once. It's nothing to do with me if Leith's having it off with Karen Swallow."

"Who says it is?" asked Paul with interest.

"No-one. I mean, Nick came on with this line about me turning her off guys for life, but he's ignorant anyway." Mark laughed. "Reckon he's only doing year 12 cause his mum couldn't stand to have him home all day on the dole."

Paul propped himself on his elbow and watched Barb carefully unwrapping her sandwiches, Mark shredding a blade of grass.

"All right," Mark burst out finally, "I was pretty shaken up when I thought Nick was talking about Cass. But I'm not against lesos as such. Fact is, I was thinking it'd be a good subject for a film."

He raved on for a while about the films he planned to make at college next year; then he started to talk himself into ringing

Cass, just to find out how she was going. Barb tried tapping her fingers, then yawning outright, but she couldn't get rid of him till the end of the lunch break.

Even then, Paul just wanted to talk about Leith.

"I s'pose I've known about her in a way," she shrugged. "She's always hanging round with Swallow these days, and she couldn't stand her before. But that doesn't prove she's a lesbian, for Christ's sake. Leith's always gone in for these intense kinds of things." *Like with Xenia, if you're so keen to know everything.*

"Why don't you ask her, if you want to find out?"

"I *don't* want to find out," said Barb, exasperated. All this talk about Leith. She wanted to talk about tonight.

But under the shower with water varnishing her breasts and belly Barb felt invincible. She raced to meet Paul at the door, and waited impatiently while Barry and Mrs O'Connell asked him questions and Paul mumbled unsatisfactory answers.

Outside they kissed deeply. Then Paul said, "So. Want to go to the pub?"

Her heart thudded. "Too noisy. Let's go and have coffee first."

They held hands across the table, but Barb's pulse was still racing, and she twitched away. "It's hot in here."

"Want to go somewhere else?"

"Do you?"

"I suggested the pub before."

"We don't seem to have the same ideas about things tonight," said Barb nastily.

"What do you mean?" asked Paul, low and clear. He stared her down till Barb wriggled in her seat and muttered, "Maybe I should just go home."

"Home? Tonight just happens to be the night when all our great sensible plans—but I suppose you've forgotten that, just like you forget everything important." Paul wiped the glare from his face. He looked into his coffee cup for a long time, then mumbled, "I'm sorry."

"I thought *you'd* forgotten," Barb said like a kid. "You kept wanting to go to the pub."

Paul held out his hand and she clutched it eagerly. "I didn't think I could say, 'Let's go straight to my place and go to bed.'"

"Well, you could."

"Well, let's."

"Did you ever get off with any of your other girlfriends?"

"Yeah, with Sunny for a while."

"Oh."

Barb turned on her side, tensing at the ache between her thighs and biting back, *Was she better than me?* Paul curled round her, his breath ruffling the hairs on the back of her neck.

"You don't have to pretend."

His arm brushed against her breasts, and the pleasure from before the pain throbbed once or twice. Barb scrambled round in a flurry of sheets and pressed her head into the curve of Paul's shoulder.

"Listen, obviously it hurt."

Barb lay still. Paul's heart ticked away under her.

"So either it's because it's your first time, or it's because I'm a clumsy goon."

She stirred. "But you've done it before."

"I could still be a clumsy goon."

Barb settled herself more comfortably on Paul's chest, smoothing the tangle of black hairs. "What was it like the first time with Sunny?"

"I was scared out of my mind and, um, not exactly the world's greatest lover. Mind you, I'm working on it."

"What about her, though?" she persisted.

"Well, it wasn't her first time."

"Oh. So this is your first time with a first time."

"Uh-huh. That's why I keep asking dumb questions."

He waited. "It hurt," Barb wailed at last.

Paul's arm tightened round her shoulder and he rocked her gently. "They reckon it gets better as you go on. What d'you think?"

Barb hunted under the pillows for a tissue. "We could always try an experiment," she said over her shoulder, and Paul's chest heaved in a long sigh.

On an impulse as she passed Leith in the corridor, Barb called out, "Haven't seen you for ages. Want to walk home tonight?"

She was hanging round outside dreaming about Paul, when all of a sudden she realised Debbie was sidling up to her. Barb stared straight ahead, jaw clenching.

"I'm not going with Claudio any more," Debbie said at last.

"Means nothing to me."

"I shouldn't have ever listened to him, y'know. I couldn't blame you if you never spoke to me again."

Barb faced her full on. "So what was he saying about me?"

"Oh, I dunno—you led him on, you were a tease, stuff like that. I wanted to believe him, see, but then it started to sink in that all he wanted was someone he could rave about you to. So I gave him the push—which, believe me, was a whole heap easier than getting up the nerve to talk to you." Debbie paused. "Barb, what did you do to him?"

"Nothing!"

Barb thought back and remembered thick dark hair, new car, sharp leather coat, not even a face, really.

"Sorry," she said to both of them.

Debbie grinned. "No worries, it cured me of thinking it was such a big deal to have a steady guy. Besides, I lost five kilos."

"You mad bastard. I've missed you."

Barb draped a friendly arm over Debbie's shoulder, and they were both grinning away like loons when Leith turned up. Barb pulled away, and Debbie went off with a cheerful wave.

"What was that all about?" Leith asked curiously.

Barb's smile widened again. "Hey, you want to hear the true story of why Claudio was such a bastard? 'Cause he was madly in love with me the whole time!"

She was racing ahead with her story when Con Theostratis yelled at them from the crowd outside the milk bar. Then it was all happening at once. Leith was stalking over, Con was cringing away in mock-terror, and Barb was still hearing the echoes of the word that had interrupted her: "Lesos!"

"Help, Gav, the leso's gonna beat us up."

"Con Theostratis, you've never been interested in me." Leith's voice floated back clearly.

"Too right, ya dog."

The group rumbled with laughter. Leith kept standing there.

"So how about you do what you want, and I do what I want?"

Jesus, thought Barb, now they'll beat *her* up. She turned slowly, in time to see the last of the guys jostling into the milk bar and hear the last of their remarks.

Leith walked back with precise steps like a soldier's. "I s'pose you know what all that was about."

"Not really."

"I've got involved with Swallow."

"What's that supposed to mean?"

"What d'you reckon? Getting off. Like Con said, we're lesos."

They walked on in silence till Leith's eyes dragged a response out of her.

"I just can't see that it's any of my business."

"So? I can still be interested in your opinion."

"I suppose I don't see why sex has to come into it. I mean, okay, you've got more friendly with Swallow, but, like, I have heaps of friends, and I don't feel as if I have to go to bed with them."

"I don't *have* to go to bed with Swallow."

"Leith, it can't go anywhere," said Barb desperately.

Leith stared back, uncomprehending. "Why not? What are you on about?"

"Look, you asked for my opinion, and I told you. If Swallow's what you want, then fine, I hope it works."

"But you don't think it will."

"Stop putting words into my mouth."

"All right, let's leave it. So," asked Leith politely, "what were you saying about Claudio?"

Barb gave a tight smile. "I'd finished. Really."

Swallow wasn't much help. "Leith, Barb and I aren't exactly best mates, what else d'you expect? And as for trying to have a debate on lesbianism with Con, in front of all his mob—you're off your face."

"Maybe I shut him up, at least."

Swallow's laugh rattled tinnily down the phone. "Con calls everyone 'leso' and 'poofter'. He's not going to stop just 'cause you *are* one. Basically, kid, you don't admit anything to people like that, you try and keep them guessing."

Leith had some more arguments, but they shuddered away in a sigh. "I wish we got more time together, Swallow."

"Well, neither of us has a car and we can't go to discos—at least both being girls means we're able to hang round in each other's rooms."

"Terrific."

"So what d'you want?"

It took till the end of her homework to get her answer ready. She wanted Barb to take an interest, like with Mark, or when she gave her that photo of Xenia. She wanted Swallow to be miserable and angry too, not all cool and worked out.

And Pam and Kylie and Jackie could fall off a cliff.

Instead, Pam came and perched on her desk next day, studying her with bird-bright eyes while she raved on about how heavy HSC was. Leith stuck to one-word answers, but after a while she started thinking hopefully that Pam might have changed.

"So how're things with you and Karen?"

"Fine."

Pam looked down confidingly. "I was sure you'd end up with Mark after him and Cass split. I heard what went on at Gav's party, even if certain people never told me." She tilted her head to one side. "I still can't see you as a lesbian, Leith."

She grinned back. "Look again."

Miss Vincini came in then, and Pam scuttled off. Glancing that way a few minutes later, Leith saw a cluster of heads, Pam, Jackie and Kylie all whispering together. Her heart caved in as she realised what she had done: told Pam everything she needed to know. Talk about suckers. Swallow would kill her for sure;

she might as well have put up an announcement on every noticeboard in Central.

Her cheek was cold, she secretly wiped away the snail-track of a tear. I'm going to pieces, Leith thought in fright, you don't cry in class. With a huge effort she managed not to, but she couldn't get as far as listening to Miss Vincini or taking notes or lifting her eyes from the blank sheet of paper in front of her.

It was like the world was suddenly booby-trapped with trip wires and water bombs, caps in her desk, rats in her locker, electric shocks in the door handles. And she wasn't even sure Swallow liked her any more.

Lonely and scared, Leith sat quietly at her desk until the kids' racket faded into the distance. Then she looked up and found Miss Vincini still waiting at the front of the class.

"You've been having a hard time of it this term, haven't you?" she asked abruptly.

Leith nodded, her teeth holding her bottom lip steady.

Miss Vincini lit a cigarette. "Normally I don't give advice to my students, on the principle that I'm paid to teach you, not mother you." She watched the curling smoke. "I just want to tell you one thing, Leith. It gets easier."

Leith shook her head a fraction, and the teacher's grey eyes crinkled behind the gold-rimmed glasses.

"Yes, I dare say you don't believe a word of it. I'd better make myself clearer. I'm trying to say that I've been through a lot of what you're going through, and I haven't regretted the choices I made. Quite the opposite."

Leith's mind stuttered over thoughts and questions as Miss Vincini went on talking. In the end all she could really handle was to say "Thanks" as she took the piece of paper from the teacher, and try to pack the rest into her smile. She gathered her books together, stood up and walked out into the bustle of the corridors.

"So is she a leso then?"

"She gave me the address of this group," said Leith.

Swallow snorted. "Which proves she knows there's a group for young lesos. Big deal. You should've asked her directly."

"I reckon she was pretty brave to say that much."

The tram glided up and they climbed in, with Swallow murmuring, "Teacher's pet," and Leith blushing.

"Anyway, you were going on before about how you shouldn't tell everyone," she retorted as they sat down.

"Not everyone, just your enemies. You can tell your friends. For instance, I haven't told my family, not in so many words, but I assume they know. Same as I assume your old man knows about you."

Leith yelped, and Swallow laughed up at her.

"I thought you told him everything," she teased.

"Well, I usually do, but he was funny about us going away, and after that . . . why *didn't* I tell him?"

"Because you've got some sense left?" suggested Swallow.

Leith smiled weakly. She sat staring out the window and chewing her thumb till Swallow nudged her.

"Wake up, Australia. We get off here."

Halfway down the tree-shadowed street, their hands clasped tightly. Halfway down the drive they turned in unison for a quick hug. Then Swallow straightened her shoulders.

"What's all the fuss about? We can always leave if we don't like it."

Leith's stomach cramped as she knocked on the door, and again and again as they waited. At last the door was opened by a half-seen figure in a huge white shirt who said, "Hi, I'm Melissa," and led them away down a long echoing corridor.

"Dracula's mansion," whispered Swallow.

Leith was choking back nervous giggles as they stepped into a bright room full of faces. There was this olive-skinned woman wearing a patterned windcheater and yellow earrings, and she was a lesbian. Everyone there was a lesbian.

"I can't believe you've never been to a gay bar before." Dani, the olive-skinned woman, slowed the car as a cat strolled across the road. "Are you two so madly in love you don't notice you're surrounded by straights?"

"Some hope."

Swallow was joking loudly with the others in the back seat.

Half an hour ago her eyes had met Leith's in a look she had never shown in public before. Leith wanted her to stop laughing and look like that again; but Dani was saying something.

"Sorry. Yeah, the meeting was great. I liked what you said about the reasons why people are so uptight about lesbianism. Where can I get those books you were talking about?"

"I'll lend them to you next meeting, if you like. Okay, here we are. Sure I can't drop you off at your place, Leith?"

"We have to say goodnight first," explained Swallow deadpan, and there was a shout of laughter and more jokes before the car drove off. Swallow stretched happily.

"Well that meeting was a waste of time — talk, talk, talk, like the parents' meetings — but things certainly warmed up when we got to the pub."

"Other way round, for me."

Swallow nudged her. "You got to loosen up, kid, learn how to have a good time."

But you didn't need to learn, and it was your first time too. Leith grabbed for comfort, and Swallow jumped back.

"Not right outside the house."

Leith followed her into the front yard, feet dragging, and stood there, head bent.

"One thing we both liked," came Swallow's voice, "and that was dancing together."

In the warm smoky music-laden room, with Swallow pulling me close as women danced together all around us.

They smiled at each other and folded smoothly into a hug, Leith's arms wrapped around Swallow's shoulders, Swallow's dark head peaceful against her breasts, their breathing stilling and slowing together.

"D'you realise," asked Leith dreamily, "that if you hadn't hung around with Trina all those years, we mightn't be here now?"

"Not her," said Swallow gruffly. "You."

All those years? Leith's heart beat faster, but she kept hold of the stillness of the moment. Swallow always tried to cover up her feelings — why couldn't she remember that? But the feelings were there. Maybe Miss Vincini was right and it was all worthwhile.

18
BY ACCIDENT

When Swallow finally remembered her, it was to dash over and ask if she was coming back to Melissa's with the rest of the gang.

"Um. I'm a bit tired."

Which was true. It was all too new, too loud, too speedy. Leith needed time to think. But she still hoped Swallow would say, "Okay, kid, let's go."

Swallow said, "Oh, right," caught a comment of Melissa's as it winged past, and swirled round to answer it. Leith stayed where she was till an arm dropped round her shoulders.

"How's things?" Dani took a closer took. "You all right, Leith?"

"Not really."

"Want to split? I don't mind driving you."

At the bar Swallow flashed a grin one way and a punch the other, wisecracking with Melissa the whole time. The music rode through the room like six-foot breakers.

"Please," said Leith.

She huddled in the front seat, knowing she could trust Dani to ask questions and draw her out.

"Okay, we have different ideas about what makes a good time. But if Swallow spends all weekend raging, when do we get to see each other? Tonight, it was like she hardly noticed I was leaving."

"So are things all right otherwise?"

"When's otherwise?" asked Leith bitterly. "Lunchtime at Central with my cousin, or tea with my father or her family? She's seen more of Melissa than me, the last few weeks."

"It happens." Dani concentrated on the road for a bit. "Like, you come along to Young Lesbians thinking you're the only one in the whole world, and suddenly there's lesos all over the place.

It figures for Swallow to go wild for a while."

"Oh yeah? Why doesn't it figure for me then?"

"Dunno. Maybe you're the quiet type. Or maybe it's just—"

Leith hurtled forward against the seat belt. Down the sweep of road ahead a car rode defiantly through beaming red lights. Two black shapes flew into the air on either side. The night rang with shock as the car sailed on to bury itself against a lamp post.

"Jesus."

One crumpled body on the median strip, another stretched out across the road.

"No, stop. You're not supposed to move them."

Standing out there in the middle of the bare black road. Terrifying but necessary. After Leith had worked out what to do if another car came hurtling at her, she had to turn and look behind her.

So small and bent, thin legs kicking away from the torn skirt at impossible angles. And her head in a puddle. Oh God.

Leith watched dizzily as Dani reversed the car back to cover them. A splotch of mud on the bumper bar was shaped like Africa. As Dani raced across to the kid on the median strip, someone groaned.

"Here's twenty cents for the phone. I got to stay with her."

Her chalk white face was scored with black scratches. She groaned again. She crushed Leith's fingers in her fist. Her eyes flickered open. By the time the ambulance came, she was screaming.

"You were amazing, staying there all that time." Dani lit another cigarette.

"Had to."

"The cops reckoned he must've realised he hit them and just thrown up his hands. He was only young—but who cares? Another jock murderer. Jesus, I'm raving, it's shock."

She reached for Leith's hand. "Mind the blood," said Leith drily.

"Oh wow. I better get you home—like I said an hour or so ago."

"Not going home. Got a spare bed at your place?"

"Sure. But—"

"Would you mind ringing my father for me?" asked Leith politely.

A puddle of blood on the road. A criss-cross of black scars. Body twisted, face dented—stop it! Mummy was killed *in* the car. But Leith could imagine how that would look too.

Somewhere in the distance, Dani moved her floppy arms, tugged at her clothes, struggled with the huge flannel nightgown. Leith stared down into a fawn whirlpool.

"Tea's strange."

"Whisky, for shock."

"Shock," Leith repeated experimentally.

A door in her memory swung open and her mother walked in, kissed her goodnight, smiled and went. Leith could hear her sobs, big deep sounds, as she watched her mother smile and go, smile and go, on the night when she never came back.

See? If you do remember her, you have to remember she's dead. Go away, Mummy, go away.

"Hey, Leith, it's okay, the ambulance guys said they'd be okay."

You could trust Dani. Relax. Maybe it's the other way round. Maybe you have to believe she's dead before you can remember her. Leith closed her eyes and studied her mother's face.

She was still shaking with cold, but they warmed each other. She woke curled against Dani's hip, her memories of the night before streaming away from her. Let them go, for now.

Dani looked down from the pile of pillows and closed her book.

"About time. Thought you'd sleep for ever. What do you want to do with the rest of the day?"

"Have breakfast."

"I meant, hang around here, or go home." She stretched brown arms, added, "You can stay if you want."

"Yeah?"

They headed for the zoo, safe as a primary school excursion, and wandered round hand in hand, checking on their favourite animals and finding new ones. When people stared, Dani would wave back, or call out, "Think we're weird? You should see the armadillos," or simply give Leith a rib-cracking hug.

"How come you're not scared?"

"Of them?" boasted Dani. She pulled a face. "Well, you figure out eventually what you can get away with — and I'm not letting anyone get away with thinking lesos are invisible."

"But what if someone saw you and told your parents, or something?"

"No-one could tell my parents anything worse than what they imagine already," said Dani with finality. "Hey, what about you, though? Didn't mean to push you into anything."

"It's fine," said Leith, gripping Dani's hand again.

Back at the house she went and crashed for a while, then woke up in electric light, wondering where she was.

"Your old man brought your school stuff round," said Dani, dumping the bag in a corner. "He seems pretty cool. Smurf came in, zonked out of her head, and he didn't bat an eyelid."

Leith struggled free of the blankets and sat up. "Dani, what *did* happen last night?"

"Did we get off, for example? How about 'sort of'?"

"Oh."

"Does it matter?"

"Well, I'm on with Swallow."

"I'd noticed." She could hear the laugh in Dani's voice and looked up to get the benefit of her warm grin. "What's the deal with you two?"

"You're kidding! Till I came to Young Lesos, I thought the same way everyone does: if you're involved with someone and you have sex with someone else, you've done something wrong. And I haven't exactly had the chance to ask Swallow her ideas on the subject lately."

Dani sat down beside her. "So what d'you think about it yourself? What if I'd said, 'Yeah, we definitely got off'? What would that do to you?"

Her dark hair wreathed her head in a thousand clusters of tight ringlets, framed a broad olive face with a wide mouth and smiling black eyes. Under her faded T-shirt Leith could follow the solid muscles of her arms and her breasts.

Excitement fizzed in her; which made it seem like a good idea to cool the conversation.

"Who knows?"

"Okay, here goes: we did get off together."

"Pity I can't remember," said Leith spontaneously.

As she clattered down the front steps next morning, she could remember everything. So, no two people were the same. You had to feel it to believe it. And the noise they had made—but then it was no-one's parents' house.

Leith wanted to pound on the door and demand to be let back into the magic circle. But she got herself away, step by step, and step by step got her closer to Central. And Swallow.

She turned the corner and nearly ran into Con Theostratis. Leith swerved to avoid him, looking stonily ahead, but he reached out and said raggedly, "Leith, I got to talk to you."

"What for?"

"It's about Gav."

"Gavin Petty?"

"Some of the kids reckoned you were with this chick who saw the accident, right?"

At first it didn't make sense. What did Gavin have to do with the accident? Then it clicked. Oh-oh. The driver. The jock murderer.

"Why would I want to talk about that mongrel?" she asked coldly.

"You *got* to tell me!" Leith raised her eyebrows, and Con looked away sullenly. "Okay, I can't make you, it's your choice." While she was trying to choose, he burst out, "He's going to die, and it's all my fault."

"Okay," Leith decided. "We can't go on standing here though."

As they walked up to the main road she started in on the story.

"Christ almighty, it looks bad for him, whatever happens," Con said with awe. "Lucky both chicks survived, or he'd really go for a row."

"How d'you know they survived?"

"Rang the hospital. The chick who was really smashed up, she's Joe Spandarakis's cousin. I met her once. Spunky little kid. I thought of sending flowers, with Gav's name on maybe, but I dunno. What d'you reckon?"

"Hard to say. I mean, would you want to know about someone who'd done that to you?"

"He didn't do it on purpose, y'know."

"He did it, y'know."

They found a huge concrete barn with some video games down the front and some old Italian guys sitting over coffees at the back. Con kept telling manic stories about Gavin till Leith butted in.

"So why'd you say it was your fault?"

" 'Cause it bloody was. Listen. We're both on the dole, then Gav gets this job at a garage. Payday, he shouts me to a night at the pub, then when he rocks up late to work the next day— whammo, he gets the shove. Okay, Saturday night he gets really wiped again. I try to grab the keys. He takes off like a bat out of hell." Con's big hands tugged at each other. "His brother's car, too, wouldn't you know it?"

Okay, Leith, you cut school for the first time ever 'cause you were curious. Now you know, what are you going to say?

"Jesus Christ, he can't die!"

Con stared round wildly, and Leith leaned forward. "Hey, who says he will?"

They argued about what the doctors had said for a while, and Con's face unknotted, muscle by muscle. Then a car's brakes squealed outside. Blood on the road, thought Leith, and I'm sitting here, trying to make a jock murderer's friend feel better. He thinks Gavin's the victim. I think the girl's the victim. So who's right?

She glanced at her watch and jumped up. "I better go."

Con followed her to the door. "Hope you don't get into trouble or anything. I just want to say, y'know, I really appreciated it." Outside he shifted feet and blurted, "Hey, and I'm sorry about yelling at you, that time."

I assumed that, the way we were talking, thought Leith; then she thought, but I'm glad he said it.

So she nodded. "Lesos aren't so bad after all, huh?"
Sounding just like Dani.

She dragged herself down the block, spinning with tiredness and
two days of unprocessed memories. Central was the same flat grey
concrete as ever, except that someone had spray-painted GAY IS
GREAT in purple near the foyer doors.

It was just on lunchtime, so Leith ditched her bag and went
over to the park. Trina had her books spread out round her as
usual, but Swallow followed her every step with a dark scowl.

"Trina, Leith and I have to talk about something."

"Off you go, then." She glanced up, said, "Leith, you look
terrible," and went placidly back to her work.

"The group go out spray-painting, hey?"

"Yeah, that's what *I* did, Saturday night. And to save you
the trouble, I can tell you I know what you did, on account of
I rang your place Sunday morning."

"That was cause of the accident." Leith explained what had
happened. "—And, yes, I did get off with Dani."

Swallow looked away. "So what's that supposed to mean about
us?"

"So what's 'us'? You've seemed more interested in Melissa than
me lately."

"Jesus, how low can you go? Melissa's my mate, kid. You
and me haven't split up, or not that I know of. If you were freaked,
why didn't you ask, instead of running off to pull this emotional
blackmail stunt?"

"Hold on. I got off with Dani cause I wanted to, not to get
at you."

Swallow's face tightened across its bones. "Well, isn't that
nice? You two should really suit. You can hold meetings in bed
about how oppressed lesbians are."

The world was pushing in on her, squeezing tighter and tighter
until she felt as if her head would burst. Leith fixed her eyes on
a single spot, Swallow's left hand. After a while she realised that
not only were Swallow's hands trembling, but her whole body.

"Swallow, if you want us to stay together, why can't you just bloody say so?"

"'Cause I can't." A small contained explosion.

She slid her hand through the grass to cover Swallow's, softly, secretly, just like in that other park ages ago, where she had sat still and longed to kiss her.

"You're the one who's big on saying things," said Swallow resentfully.

"Okay then. I don't want us to split up, just because I got off with Dani. I happen to love you, Swallow."

Now Swallow looked at her, a tough guarded hopeful trusting look.

"Me too."

I keep forgetting the way she covers her feelings. I keep wishing she didn't. All those years. Does she realise I'm not saying I won't get off with Dani again? I could hurt her. I do hurt her.

"Your friend seems very reliable—does she work as a nurse? She told me that you'd coped well with the accident, but then had bad shock afterwards, so it seemed better for you to stay where you were. Do you feel all right now?" asked Mr Dunbar with concern.

"Fine. Dani was great."

"I can understand your reaction. One of my students had an epileptic fit once, and the rest of us were almost as shaken as he was. Other people's suffering's always hard to bear."

Leith went on listening and nodding, while part of her yelled voicelessly: But what about *your* accident? What about Mummy? What about me getting off with Dani? How do I ever get all that into the conversation?

The doorbell rang, and she sat chewing at her thumb until her father came back, eyebrows slightly raised.

"It's a strange young man. He says he wants to see you." He stood guard behind her as Leith went cautiously to the door.

"Con. What's happened?"

"Listen, I didn't mean to interrupt or nothing, just thought you'd like to know—" his grin burst through—"Gav's gonna make it."

"Hey, that's great." Leith's hands shot out and Con pulled her into a bear hug. "Bloody great," she gasped as he whirled her round. "Con, that's just *great*." She was gulping and sniffing, and he was nodding eagerly, both still locked close in happy relief.

Behind them Mr Dunbar cleared his throat carefully. "Perhaps your friend would like some coffee, Leith. Or a beer, maybe."

Con was already backing away, "No, thanks," he mumbled. "I got to go."

Leith felt like a row of iron filings swayed between two magnets. As Con clanged the iron gate shut, she ran over and called, "Thanks for letting me know."

"No probs. See you round."

And he swung off, looking big and easy and confident, even if he felt differently inside. I wish he could've come in and talked for a while, thought Leith, watching him disappear round the corner. I wish . . . She went back into the house to find Mr Dunbar.

Going down the hallway she heard echoes of her father's voice. "People get hurt all the time. Why shouldn't they be allowed to feel hurt?" Leith blew her nose and scrubbed the tears from her eyes. *We're sort of careful with each other about everything, him and me.*

She walked into the kitchen. Quickly, before she could scare again, she said, "Dad, there's something I should've told you before. I'm a lesbian."

19
LOVE AND FRIENDSHIP

Debbie dropped into the desk beside her. "Saw Silv at the weekend."

"How is she?" asked Barb guiltily.

"Fat as a pig, and pig-miserable."

"Oh, hell."

Mrs Simons came in then, and Barb had a whole period to work out exactly how long it was since she had seen Silv. Basically, not since she had been going with Paul. He thought Silv and Craig were boringly conventional, and Silv thought he was too way out. Barb thought she was somewhere in the middle, as usual.

"So why's Silv so miserable?" she asked Debbie as they walked over to the park.

"Oh, you know. Craig's at work, we're at school, her friends on the dole can't get out to the sticks to see her, she can't get in to see them. All that sort of thing."

"Oh, wow. I should go over this weekend."

"Go where?" asked Paul from behind them.

"Silvana's."

"Jesus, what for?"

Barb looked him in the eye. " 'Cause she's my friend, like Mark's yours."

She was getting her arguments together. It's not just to help her, it's 'cause I don't want to end up isolated myself. I need my friends, Paul, as well as you.

But Paul just laughed. "Point taken. How about I see Mark when you're seeing Silvana, and then everyone's happy. Only not *this* weekend—George's got that beach house, and he's invited us along."

"Sun, surf and sex," Debbie sighed.

Barb stopped, shirt half unbuttoned, to watch Paul undress: the muscles roping his long pale arms, charcoal shading of hair on his long pale chest, the darker bunch of genitals at his narrow hips. He caught her staring and grinned.

"Voyeur. It's your turn now."

She attacked her buttons as briskly as if she was at the doctor's, but his admiring eyes slowed her down.

"You've got a beautiful body."

"Truly?"

"Come here and I'll show you."

"This is beautiful," said Paul, rounding her breast and lifting her nipple. "This is beautiful," ruffling crisp curls. He knelt and drew his hands the full length of her body. "This is beautiful."

"Truly? Truly," Barb said, satisfied.

He leaned into her and they sighed together. Their bodies made little sucking sounds as they met and parted. Paul lifted his head to look down at her, dark and concentrated. Other times he sort of shambled, but here he was like a dancer. And she was the only one who knew.

Barb gasped as she took up his movements, changed them, faster, slower, until all at once the dance had its own definite rhythm and they were following it together, wildly and breathlessly, till everything vanished into a blaze of no words that left Barb clinging tightly to Paul and repeating, "Yes, yes, yes, yes, yes."

I almost said I loved him, she realised. I wonder if he was trying not to say it too.

They lay there in a tangle of arms and legs. Out of a complicated thought about making love sometimes feeling as if you were actually *making* something, Barb said, "You can see why people decide to have kids."

Paul freed himself carefully and moved to the far side of the bed, where he started to roll a cigarette slowly and precisely.

"Hey, what did I say?"

"I *do not* want to have kids."

"I didn't say you did."

"Well, that's what it sounded like."

The words bickered back and forth. Then all at once Paul was swinging on her with a hunted glare, then burying his head in his hands. Barb waited a moment, her heart beating fast, before she touched his arm.

"Paulie. It's just a dumb fight."

"To you." His voice echoed through his fingers.

"What is it to you?"

"My family." A long sigh. "Always fighting. You've seen Xeens—well, she's a beginner compared to the rest. I hated it, I used to throw up. But then I lose my temper like this, and I hate myself too."

"Everyone loses their temper sometimes. Silv and Craig used to have a ding-dong row every weekend, reckoned they liked making up."

She leaned back, deliberately relaxed, and watched Paul start to think about it.

"Yeah? Wonder if Mum and Dad were like that. Nah, they can't have been, they were too bloody lethal."

"Truly? When I've been to your place, they seem kind of quiet and ordinary."

He nodded. "I'm not sure if they decided to make the best of things, or if they just ran out of steam. Either way, Mum retired—it's Dad and Xenia and George who do the screaming these days."

Barb grinned, and he smiled up in surprise. "You make it all seem pretty ordinary," he told her. "Hey, how about we try some of that making up you were talking about before?"

"Good idea."

Barb slid into sleep with a contented sigh. When she woke, it was the middle of the night. Paul was sitting up, pushing his head against the wall.

"What?" she said from a drowsy fog.

He didn't answer for a while, and Barb drifted away again.

"*Mama*'s crying," came a flat voice. "She says she wants a divorce, but *Baba* won't let her."

Barb jerked into wakefulness. Talking in his sleep, she realised half a beat later.

"What if Barb and I are wrong for each other?" droned the voice. "I couldn't bear it."

She reached up and pulled him back into the warm lair of the bedclothes. His sleep-sweaty skin stuck to hers, she combed his matted curls with her fingers.

"We'll be all right, Paulie, we'll be right."

"I love you," mumured Paul as his body relaxed heavily against her. Barb lay awake for a while, weighed down with thinking, and woke again with the dawn.

The house was quiet. She let herself out into a milky-blue morning and started to run.

Help.

At the bottom of the hill the new-washed beach glittered before her, the sea making sleek lacy patterns down one side. Barb slowed to a walk. So what was the big panic?

He *wants* us to go wrong. It's not fair, making me say it'll be all right. I can't make it work all by myself, not if he's dead set on wrecking everything.

Her eyes clenched tight on tears and her heart pounded. The morning whirled away, leaving Barb to the black nights after Claudio had gone. She paced down the beach in a trance of misery.

No-one else had trodden the pale orange sand yet. As Barb walked on she started to notice small broken shells, bits of sand-crumbed jellyfish, dashes of bright pink seaweed. She tried again.

Paul's like Leith, complicated. But I could always handle Leith.

If I'd really wanted the he-man type, I could've stuck with Claudio. And he turned out to be pretty kinky anyway, the way he treated Deb.

So—

All at once Barb was starving. She turned back, thinking about eggs on toast, planning how she would wake Paul. But, most of all, suddenly and sharply missing Leith.

I hope I get to tell her one day how stupid I was, getting all steamed up about that leso stuff. I mean, you need your friends.

Paul was sitting on the front step with a bowl of cornflakes. He looked up and smiled, his black eyes soft and clear in his tired face.

"God, I had serial nightmares about my bloody family. Hope

I didn't wake you up."

"No problem." And lucky she had decided not to stack on a turn about something he clearly didn't remember saying.

Suddenly Paul filled her mind. Paul in the distance, derro overcoat flapping. Paul in close up, smiling or blank or thoughtful or freaked or deeply intent as he leaned over her. Paul sitting on the front step, eating cornflakes.

"I love you, you know that."

He ditched the bowl and held out his arms, mumbling something as she leaned against him.

"Huh?"

"I said, I love you too. Heaps."

So everything was okay, after all.

Barry dropped his arm round her shoulder, while Sue snuggled at his other side.

"We've had our troubles, I know, but I can say for certain that I look forward to getting two lovely new daughters in June."

Practising for the wedding speeches, Barb sneered automatically. Actually, she still couldn't believe it. The whole thing had been dragging on forever, and she had basically decided it would never happen.

And now there was a real live date . . . All the same, she still couldn't make herself believe it.

Over lunch she found herself halfway to a slanging match with Barry over test tube babies, but he cooled the whole thing brilliantly, and the anxious look faded from Mrs O'Connell's eyes. Barb hated him even more. For years Barry had kept her mother dangling and Barb had had to look after her. And now he had the nerve to turn round and protect her mother from her.

In the meantime her mother was glowing with joy and kept reaching for Barry's hand. Barb muttered some excuse and went to her room, where she perched numbly on the edge of the bed.

So there I'll be in a posh house in the suburbs, while he lords it over us and I miss my friends. Like Paul. God, what if he tries to stop me seeing Paul?

She was still sitting there neatly, counting the silver cups, when she heard a gentle tap on the door. Barb shook herself and called, "Come in."

"I thought you might like some coffee," said Mrs Hartwell. She set the cup down carefully and looked round the bungalow. "Well, it's worked out very nicely having you here, all things considered."

"Mm," Barb agreed past the lump in her throat.

"Now, your grandfather and I had a little talk about whether it was wise for you to change schools in your final year. As Colin says, you're always welcome here, so I had a word with Sandra and Barry, and—"

Buried in her pillow, Barb was sobbing her heart out, while her grandma patted her shoulder and chirped comfort to her.

I didn't know I had a choice. If I do, I can't go. But this way I'll miss Mum, so much. Jesus, I'll even miss Sue.

She wept harder.

Everyone seemed to think it was sensible to stay with her grandparents, but Barb still needed to check it out five times a day.

"But if you've decided, what else is there to say?" asked Debbie impatiently.

"Well, it's a big step, not living with your folks."

"You'll be back with them next year."

"Yeah, right."

Barb mumbled goodbye and ducked into the library, wishing she could say out loud to someone that she wouldn't be living with her mum next year either. She was *never* going to live with Barry—and that meant she could hardly expect him to steer her through teachers college or get her a job if she flunked out.

Still, that was all right, Barb thought, scanning the titles in the careers section. Mr Hansen had liked her new idea. You could see him making a note to report to Ms Lee that he had encouraged higher ambitions in a girl student. But he could only tell Barb that it was possible. She still needed someone who could tell her whether she would really be able to handle it.

It was like ESP, how Leith came wandering down the tunnel of library shelves, off in a dream as usual, so that Barb had plenty of time to work out opening lines that covered the months when they had hardly spoken to each other. But, face to face with Leith, she just blurted out, "D'you reckon I could be an architect?"

Leith's smooth forehead wrinkled in a frown. Then she grinned. "It'd have to be better than ending up back at school again. Where'd you get the idea from, anyway?"

Barb couldn't answer back for a moment, because she was too busy grinning back.

20
BARB AND LEITH

They got to the pub late and laughing.

Debbie winked as she danced past. "What kept you two—as if we couldn't guess?"

Then Silvana waved frantically, and Barb dug Paul in the ribs. "Be nice, okay?"

"Dunno what to say to doting parents." Paul made a face. "Oh well, at least this way I don't have to hold the kid or anything."

Cool Fools' guitars roared suddenly, drowning any chance of an answer. Barb's heart beat faster. She wanted to leap onto the nearest table, throw her arms wide and belt out a song to the whole room. It was great to be back, great to forget about study for a night and have the first term holidays ahead.

"Look, there's that Nina who came to the group last week. She seems a bit lost. Come on."

Pushing through the crowd behind Dani's sturdy back, Leith confessed to herself that she would have just felt sorry for Nina from a distance. She admired Dani all over again. But even Dani couldn't get Nina to talk. She watched them warily from small bright eyes, shutting her mouth like a trap on "yes" and "no".

"Been to the pub before?" asked Dani in desperation.

"No."

"You're brave," sighed Leith. "I nearly freaked right out, my first night at Young Lesos, and I'd gone along with someone else, too. Walked in, took one look at this woman, thought, 'God, she's a *lesbian*', and nearly ran home again. That was you," she added to Dani.

Dani grinned. "Hope you're not going to make a habit of running away from me."

Then she stopped short, because Nina was squeezing out a tiny smile and muttering, "Know what you mean."

"Yeah?" said Leith encouragingly. She and Dani leaned forward to catch Nina's soft voice, and their three heads enclosed a circle of quiet in the pub's racket.

Outside the kitchen window the afternoon sun outlined every green leaf. Barb stretched comfortably.

"Wow. I'm glad we're talking again. So tell me, what's the latest on your dad?"

"He's fine with me, as far as I can see, but he gets pretty twitchy if I so much as mention Swallow."

As Leith frowned, Barb said warmly, "Hey, I reckon that's great, for starters anyway."

"Huh." Leith slapped the lids on two piled sandwiches. "People adjust to all sorts of things. So he might as well start getting used to Swallow."

"Meaning she'll be around for a while?"

"Good question. I mean, I like Dani, we have these great raves; and then me and Swallow, we've been through heaps together." Leith bit her thumb. "What would you do, if you were me?"

"Enjoy it," Barb said promptly. "I never got to choose between two guys I really fancied."

"But I don't want to *choose*."

"That's the way it is, kid."

"Not necessarily. Some people have more than one serious relationship at a time."

"Then some people make two other people miserable."

"So it's better to choose, and just make one other person miserable?"

"Hey, stop it. This is way over my head," Barb grinned. "Y'know, twelve months ago I used to think you were this total innocent. Jesus!"

"Well, twelve months ago I thought being a lesbian meant being lonely for life. Some hope! Mind you, twelve months ago I would've been in a real state over some hassle a quarter the size of this one. You must've thought I was a hopeless wimp."

"Hardly," said Barb through a mouthful of sandwich. "Half the kids I knew were terrified by the way you talked—Silv, for example. Even me, sometimes."

"Yeah?" Leith sat up and started to demand examples.

She was moving into Paul's arms for a slow number when Xenia pranced up, trailing a wispy guy with a fashion haircut and a bewildered look.

"This is Damien from the theatre group. I'm showing him how the other half lives," she screeched. "We're at Mark's table, if you can bear to tear yourselves apart."

She whirled them off and they sat round trading news, while Cass watched Mark surreptitiously, and Mark directed all his comments at Paul or Xenia. Don't know why he worked so hard at getting Cass back, when he just ignores her, thought Barb, deciding to go to the loo.

On her way she caught sight of Silvana, sitting by herself, shoulders slumped. I'll go and cheer her up afterwards, Barb told herself. But as she weaved back through the crowd, waving and calling to friends, a hand reached out and stopped her.

Swallow went by, cheek to cheek with Melissa in a parody of a waltz. Nothing had changed. Leith wanted to burst into tears and run . . . to Dani, which was a bit suspect.

The track finished and Dani leaned over. "Go on, ask your girlfriend for a dance."

"Aren't you her girlfriend?" asked Nina, surprised.

"Well . . ." Their eyes met in a long look, then Dani gave her a push towards the dance floor.

Walking across the polished boards, Leith felt large and noticeable. She wished she could skip ahead and find out what happened in the end. No such luck. It was all up to her and Dani and Swallow, of course. She had to make her own rules. Just like I always wanted to, thought Leith ironically.

Swallow was waiting for her, hands in pockets.

"Want to dance?"

"Why not?" said Swallow off-handedly. Then she added a sideways grin.

"My dad—Neil—I'm calling him Neil from now on. Neil says he's commissioning you to design his retirement home. Not that he's retiring yet; you get to practise first."

"Tell him not to hold his breath," said Barb morosely. "Turns out, once Mum's married to Barry's money, I won't be eligible for a government handout."

"Barry should give you an allowance then."

"He probably would—he's completely sold on the idea of me doing architecture. The question is, would I take it?"

"It's just money, Barb."

"No, it isn't." Barb tugged hard on a lock of hair as she waited for the words. "Look, I changed from teaching 'cause I didn't want to be under Barry's thumb. So if I let him pay my way . . ."

Leith frowned in silence till Barb prodded her.

"Well, Neil's paying my way. Even though it'll be heaps easier for me to see Swallow when I'm living in college. Do you think I should refuse?"

"No way. That just proves what I've been saying: he's an okay guy. Besides, I'd rather take an allowance from Mum, no worries—except that on what she earned, I *was* eligible for government money."

"Where on earth will you get the money from, then?"

"A little thing called work."

"Oh, right." Leith blushed.

"The way I see it, I can either get a job and study part-time; study and work part-time; or give study a great big miss."

"Give it a miss?" repeated Leith, round-eyed. "You can't do that!"

Barb swivelled her chair round on its back legs. "Oh, I dunno, Leith. I keep thinking, if Barry reckons architecture's such a smart move, maybe it'll turn me into someone like him . . . It's all a mess. I wish I could just do what I wanted without having to think about it."

"I wish I could just *know* what I want without having to think about it."

"Yeah. That's what I mean."

"Claudio. Haven't seen you in ages," said Barb automatically.

Over Claudio's shoulder she had noticed Xenia and Mark heading for the dance floor. Xenia twined her long arms round Mark's neck, and he laughed and leaned forward to whisper in her ear. Barb's eyes widened.

"So how've you been?"

"Fine. How about you?"

As Claudio started to tell her in detail, she watched Mark and Xenia closely. *Funny, I thought she was gay. Well, it doesn't prove anything, Leith having a crush on her—or maybe it doesn't prove anything, her flirting with Mark. Poor Cass, either way.*

"Sorry, Claudio, I missed the last bit."

"I said, it looks like I'll get a transfer after all, if our new head of department—"

"Fantastic."

Suddenly she couldn't stand it a moment longer. To think that she had ever sat around breaking her heart over this boring nerd. With a muttered excuse, Barb plunged into the crowd, ducking between dancers and pushing through conversations, frantic to find any gap in the wall of bodies that kept her from Paul.

"You were having a fine old time, yakking away with Dani."

Leith wanted to snap back, well, you were having a fine old time, cheek-to-cheeking with Melissa. But it was reasonable for Swallow to feel jealous of Dani, and it wasn't reasonable for her to feel jealous of Melissa. She watched Swallow bopping away, neat and fast, and felt like she was trying to dance in gumboots.

"God, you're a hopeless dancer," commented Swallow at that precise moment. Leith's mouth twitched, and her body clamped even tighter. "It's a fact, kid, that's all."

To her own fury, Leith's eyes started to glaze over with tears. Swallow gave an exaggerated sigh.

"Oh well. I'll just have to teach you then."

With Swallow's arms folded light and firm around her, Leith could follow the music after all. Her hand gripped Swallow's shoulder; Swallow pulled her closer. After a while she bent and murmured, "We're doing all right, aren't we? At everything, I mean, not just dancing."

Swallow's impatient nod, Swallow's sharp green eyes said that maybe she agreed, but she didn't see why Leith always had to put it into words.

"Listen, you might think this is really dopey . . ."

"I'm listening."

"It's just that I keep wondering, d'you reckon you could be a lesbian 'cause of your mum dying?"

Leith's grin disappeared. "Like you go for guys 'cause your dad pissed off?" Barb's face stiffened, and Leith stared out the window, muttering, "Well, why should we have to explain me and not you?"

"It has an effect on me too, you being gay."

Leith turned back, startled. "How?"

Barb was neatly pleating the tablecloth. "I'll probably make a mess of this too, but—well, Debbie, she knows lesbians *exist*, but she'd never apply it to her. Me, I'm your friend, I talk to you, I *have* to think about things. I mean, why d'you reckon I was so freaked when you told me?" She looked up and smiled. "I s'pose I'm complaining 'cause now I know I'm, like, heterosexual, whereas Deb and Silv, they still just think the whole world's like them."

"Well, it's not," said Leith, but she was smiling too. "Hey, on the subject of hets, how're you and Paul going?"

"Good. No exciting dramas, not like some people, but I reckon it'll last."

"Jesus, I can't imagine past the end of this week!"

"Well, that makes sense," Barb told her. "I've been going with guys for years, and you're just starting out, really. Stands to reason you won't have some great ten-point plan of what you want. I mean, even looking back at Claudio, I think I was bloody ignorant then."

Leith shook her head. "I'll always be friends with Swallow, whatever happens."

"So you say. No-one, but no-one, stays friends after they bust up."

"Swallow still goes bushwalking with Jan. Dani shares a house with her first lover. Melissa and Helen—"

"Maybe it's different if you're both girls," said Barb doubtfully.

Once she got to Paul, the urgency dropped away. She leaned against his side and listened while he argued about painting with Damien, until Cass got Damien up to dance. Then they turned to each other in a long quiet look that drowned out the rattle of glasses, the babble of voices, the throb of the band.

Katie Watson swayed past with a sultry glance in Paul's direction, and Barb felt a distant pang. What would I do without him? Just 'cause I'm not here with Claudio, or someone like Mark, how do I know I'm safe? There's too many things that can go wrong.

Mum, falling asleep in front of the TV; setting her hair slowly and carefully every weekend. Mum going off alone to the office party, her mouth sad under the neat lipstick. Mum, the ghost in the oatmeal facepack.

Ah, cool it, Barb told herself. Maybe Paul will love you forever. Maybe you'll be this hot-shot architect, too busy to notice if there's a guy around. Or just maybe you'll finally get it into your skull that your Mum's not exactly lonely, she's about to get married again, and *she's* rapt in Barry, even if you're not.

Out on the dance floor, Debbie was thoughtfully eyeing the drummer over her partner's shoulder. Con Theostratis loomed over a group of year 10 girls. Silvana and Craig clung together. Cass and Mark and Xenia and Damien danced in an uneasy foursome.

Leaning against Paul, watching the changing patterns as the colour wheel turned from yellow to purple to red to green, Barb sighed happily.

"Everyone's here tonight."

Except Leith, of course.

The opening bars of the latest hit song, "She's A Treasure", were the signal. All the kids from Young Lesbians met in the middle of the dance floor.

"Everybody ready?" yelled Swallow, and they started to sing their own version.

> She's a leso—what d'you say?
> She's a leso—I say it's okay.
> She's a leso—worth her weight in go-o-old.

Melissa's cheeky grin, Dani's slow smile, Nina's eyes widening and Swallow conducting the whole thing, her pale face flushed bold and beaming. And all around the room women staring at the linked circle of dancers, laughing and starting to join in. Leith loved everyone . . .

. . . like in that moment on the river. So that's what it had all been about, wanting the Edwardians, wanting another world, somewhere to belong.

> She's a leso—gettin' me keen.
> She's a leso—she can be mean.
> She's a leso—very nice to ho-o-old.

Laughing with Swallow, laughing with Dani, Leith still kept on thinking, was it just a waste of time, all that Edwardian stuff? Pining after Xenia, never noticing Swallow. But without the Edwardians she would never have written Emily Lydia Mather's story, and Emily Lydia was real. Real and dead, like her mother.

I'll never get to tell her how Swallow's jokes fit in here, mourned Leith. I'll never get to tell her how Dani's deep black eyes notice everything. But then, let's face it, I'm still working on saying that kind of thing to my father—to Neil.

At least I can talk to Barb again these days.

"It's practically identical," Leith said excitedly. "Claudio for you and Xenia for me, sort of glittering prizes, and then Paul and Swallow, the kids next-door. And you questioning about Barry and me about Neil, and both worrying about what we want to do and what groups we fit into. Exactly the same things have happened to both of us."

"Yeah, but . . . not really, though."

"Why?"

"'Cause you're gay and I'm not."

"So? We're both people."

Barb looked obstinate. "But things, outside things, are different for us. Truly, Leith. Me and Paul will always be treated differently from you and Swallow. It has to have an effect."

Leith shrugged. "Perhaps. Oh well, I'm glad you warned me I'd turn into a leso if I kept raving on about Xenia. Otherwise I might've taken even longer to sort myself out."

"Lay off." Barb wriggled in her chair. "I've said I'm sorry about that. I was going through a bad—"

"Just teasing," said Leith with a wicked grin. "Want to know the other thing I'm glad about?"

"Maybe."

"I'm glad we're still friends."

"Couldn't agree more," said Barb wholeheartedly.

They kept on talking; the sun kept shining green through the trees; the world outside kept moving on.